Loxley Belle

Book Four

Ghosts of Summerleigh Series
By M.L. Bullock

Dedication

For all the younger sisters.

Shadows

Gray, cold and gray
Is the desolate wintry sky.
As the colorless daylight fades away
And the starless night draws nigh,
I sit in my darkened room
By the fire,—it is burning low,
While fancy weaves in her pauseless loom,
And swift and silent, amid the gloom.
Her shuttle glides to and fro.
Sad, sombre and sad
Is the web that she weaves to-night;
And it wraps my soul as the world is clad
In the desolate evening light.
Strange is this nameless sorrow!
I weep, and I scarce know why
It is the frown of some dark to-morrow
That looms above me, and I must borrow
Grief from by and by?
Why, fancy why
Hast done so ill thy task?
Instead of a gloom like the starless sky,
Oh, give me the thing I ask,
It is just as easy to rear
A sunny castle in Spain
As to conjure up some faith or fear,
Some shadowy grief that brings a tear
From the ache of a nameless pain.
Ellen P. Allerton, 1835-1893

Prologue—Loxley Belle

Desire, Mississippi, May 1954

My walk through the overgrown woods behind Summerleigh never prepared me for the sad sight I knew I would see when I finally cleared the last hill. Summerleigh rose high, as high as she ever had, but she was empty. There was no life in her anymore because there were no more Belles living under her roof. The sight of the crumbling old home, all quiet and empty, weighed on me even though it had been nigh on ten years since I lived here. Aunt Dot, Harper and I moved out shortly after Addison's wedding. That had been a happy event. Throwing rice at Addison and her husband had seemed a strange thing to do, but I'd been delighted at her happiness. I cried when we sent them off to Fort Lauderdale for their honeymoon. Daddy had been watching too from the staircase, but he didn't come too close. He'd attended Addison's wedding as a silent witness; I never saw Jeopardy, and I was glad for that.

Yes, I had been back to Summerleigh many times since we'd moved out, but Aunt Dot never knew about any of my visits. She never caught on that I was breaking into the family home and walking the empty halls pining for days gone by. I hated keeping secrets from Aunt Dot, but she wouldn't understand and I couldn't tell her. The Ghost Boy followed me around but didn't want to play with me anymore. I was too grown for that, I suppose. Or maybe he knew what a horrible sinner I'd become. A simply terrible soul. But I couldn't help myself. I tried, but I couldn't stop. This horrible secret was mine to bear alone. Everyone else in this family had secrets, so why not me? I was a Belle, after all; it was kind of expected of me, as all the kids at school reminded me every day. Especially Shannon Bohannan.

"Would you look at that dress? Where does she buy her clothes? The Five and Dime? She's about as exciting as home-churned butter. Come on, Betty Lou. You wouldn't want Crazy Belle's bad taste to rub off on you."

Crazy Belle. That's what she called me. Like it was a big joke. But I was home now. And here amongst the odd shadows and the peeling wallpaper, I belonged. Why had we ever moved? *One day, this place will be mine. And I will make it grand for you, Daddy. I will!*

Aunt Dot bought a house in Lucedale that had all the modern conveniences, which she was very proud of. "Loxley dear, we can have whatever kind of furnishings we like. We are not poor, not at all. How about this sweetheart bedroom set for your room? It has a lovely tufted couch for you and your friends to sit on and read your magazines. You need a radio too." At first, it seemed a wise thing to have a new home with all the "modern conveniences," but after a few years, the longing to return home to Summerleigh had not dissipated. I wasn't afraid of the ghosts. I loved them all. Well, most of them. I didn't love the Ghost Boy with the dead eyes or the girl who wore a blood-soaked dress and moaned in the attic from time to time. Despite these occasional unwanted visitors, I yearned for home. I missed the fireplace that smoked, the damp-smelling rooms and the creaking floor treads on the stairs. And I missed the orchard of peach trees behind Summerleigh and the wild tangle of rose vines in the overgrown front yard that always hid a new litter of kittens. I had a terrific time hiding those poor mewling animals from Momma.

Those had been happy days before Jeopardy disappeared.

Before Daddy died so suddenly.

Before Momma lost her mind.

I eased open the screen door; it made a shrill, squeaking sound as I went inside. Birds were nesting on the back porch. They added to the squeaking to voice their complaints before fleeing from my presence. *Mind the floor, Loxley.* I had to be careful right here. The floor had weakened a bit. I stepped over the doorjamb and into the kitchen. The door closed with a thud behind me as I walked into my favorite room in the house. I could almost imagine Harper at the stove and Momma on the phone talking to Augustine Hogue about one person or the other. I pictured Jeopardy sulking in the doorway, her wild hair unbrushed; her expression, as always, both sad and angry. And Addison? Where would she be? She would be blowing her nose in the other room. We weren't allowed to blow our noses in front of Momma or in the presence of any company we might have. Not even Miss Augustine, who had been a fixture at our house for so long, had ever witnessed any of the Belle girls blowing their noses in public.

Of course, these austere rules were relaxed somewhat when Daddy came home. Until he left on one of his many adventures. Miss Augustine agreed with Momma on everything to a T. *Yes, Loxley. Blowing your nose in public is a very vulgar thing to do. And whistling, too. Ladies don't do either of those things.* I whistled as I peeked out the screen door to make sure no one had followed me. I couldn't think why, but I had the feeling that someone *was* watching me.

And not a dead someone. A living someone.

I scanned the tree line as best I could, but I didn't see anyone from my vantage point at the back door. *Huh, there's nothing to see, silly girl. Now take your walk and go home before you're found out.* I sighed as I walked into the parlor. The leaky roof had finally fallen in, just as Momma prophesied all those years ago. An entire corner of the parlor was covered in a landslide of rotting wood, shingles and chipped paint. My heart sank at the sight of time's destructive powers. Poor Daddy never had a chance to bring this place back to life, and the restoration of Summerleigh had been his dream.

I could easily imagine Momma's disapproving voice in my ear. *One day that roof will be the death of us all, JB. This old house is going to crumble around us, and you wouldn't care at all if we died here in this rotting disaster. I hate this house.*

I couldn't remember Daddy's answer. He mostly didn't take Momma seriously when she said things like that. He would smile and wink at us girls behind her back, which always made us snigger. And we'd pay for that when he left again. Momma knew what we were doing. He always left too soon, and although we Belles missed him—we sobbed for days after he left—we didn't speak a word against him. We all understood that Momma could be a handful. It was an unspoken understanding we girls had that Daddy had to leave for a while on occasion. Who wouldn't want to escape the madness that sometimes erupted in our home?

Except for Jeopardy. She never wanted Daddy to leave; she wrote him almost every day. I'd been too little to write him letters or send postcards. But from time to time, when Jeopardy asked, I would ask her to write a few things. Other times, I would draw him a picture and Jep would include it with her letter. And in all those drawings, he was at home at Summerleigh with all of us. I was always careful to add Momma to the drawing, though. She didn't like being left out, and most of the time she read Jeopardy's letters before she allowed my sister to send them.

Best leave the parlor, Loxley Grace. Too many memories in this room.

"Daddy? Are you here? It's me, Loxley."

He didn't answer me back, but that had been his voice. I waited a few minutes, just in case he had something else to say. Sometimes ghosts were slow to communicate, but he used to always come see me. Always.

Heavens above! He must know my secret! He knows about me and is ashamed of me.

"Oh, Daddy. Please don't hide from me," I half-sobbed as I waited in the musty parlor.

I heard nothing and saw no one. I sighed as I began to make my way upstairs. My footsteps on the staircase resonated too loudly, reminding me that I was all alone. Usually, that comforted me. But not this afternoon.

We all believed that Daddy would make this place a palace. Jeopardy believed in his dream most of all. Those two were like two peas in a pod. Daddy loved all us Belles, but I think sometimes he loved Jeopardy better than anyone else. I didn't begrudge her that extra love; besides, Daddy had plenty of leftover love for the rest of us too. No, I didn't hate my sister on account of it. She got so little love from Momma that she deserved extra helpings from our father. I tried to explain this to Addison once, but she got so excited that she developed a nosebleed right then and there. Or so she thought. It was actually the Ghost Boy that liked making Addison sick all the time. He'd tweak her nose, squeeze her throat. I told her so, but she never believed me. Momma certainly didn't believe any of my stories, as she liked to call them.

Momma did not have the ability to see the good in anything that did not come in a Woolworth's shopping bag. She had high standards, to be sure. Too high for anyone to measure up to, least of all John Jeffrey Belle and his girls. Despite this awareness, I missed Momma, and I knew I was the only one who did. That was a heavy load to bear. Yes, I missed the coolness of her hands when she touched my feverish forehead and the occasional kind word she sent my way. I easily summoned up the gentle smiles she showered on me when I did everything just right. Like not wet the bed and brush my own hair and polish my teeth with baking soda after a good brushing. But even in those moments, when everything fell into place and I remembered when to smile, when to speak and when to stop drinking water for the night, there was always the presence of icy fear.

Fear that Momma would disappear and all that would remain would be the monster of my nightmares. A wild, screaming banshee with smeared lipstick, crooked bobby pins and sweaty skin.

And the transformation happened so quickly that it always took my breath away.

But I forgive you, Momma. I forgive you and I love you.

I felt a little sick as I pulled the bracelet out of my pocket and scurried off to the nursery. The dead boy wasn't in here, thankfully. But most of the time, whenever he was at Summerleigh, he was in this room. I absently wondered where ghosts went when they weren't haunting me. And why just me and no other Belle? What had I done to deserve such morbid "friends"? And where would I go when I died?

I walked to the far closet and knelt down. The wood felt grimy beneath my knees. My fingers expertly pried the loose board up, and I set it aside. With a quick glance around the bare room, I lifted the cigar box from the floor and opened it. I had so many treasures in this box; I would have to find another box soon. And another hiding place. This would make six treasure boxes hidden around Summerleigh. I held the gold bracelet up to the light and admired it before depositing it in its new home. Strangely enough, I did not feel one shred of regret while doing it. But I should. I should feel regret. I closed the box and put it back in its hiding place. Replacing the board, I climbed to my feet and ducked out of the closet as I dusted off my knees. Oh, now I felt it. Yes, my familiar friends Guilt and Shame were here. They covered me like a heavy quilt—they weighed down my already-heavy soul. I would never get to heaven with a soul so heavy.

What a horrible thing to do, Loxley Belle! Just horrible! What would your Daddy say?

"I know, Momma. I know! I'm sorry!" I said to the dead air around me.

But Momma wasn't here, and she wasn't dead. This was my own conscience accusing me of these terrible crimes. No, Momma was very much alive at the asylum, but I wasn't supposed to talk about that. I was supposed to pretend that Aunt Dot and I were as happy as two clams. We were the peas in the pod now. Not because she wanted it to be that way but because it just was. Why couldn't she understand that I needed to talk about Momma? I couldn't remember much about my mother anymore, and I felt that I should. Poor Momma, locked away in an insane asylum for the rest of her life. I wondered if she ever thought about Harper or Addison or me. I wondered if she could think of anything except herself. She never could before. Did they have medicine for that? That's what Aunt Dot said about Momma one of the few times she would talk about her. *She's in a better place and getting the medicine she needs, Loxley dear.* Momma's birthday was coming up, and I wanted to go see her. Maybe bring her a small gift or a card to cheer up her bedroom.

But it was more than that. More than just wanting to cheer Momma up. I wanted to see her because I had to know. I had to see if my greatest fear was truly possible. Was I going to become a monster too? I had the makings of one, that was for certain. But Aunt Dot wouldn't even entertain the idea of my visiting Momma, and Harper agreed with her.

I'd brought the subject up again to Aunt Dot last night at dinner. "The only thing you can give your mother is your prayers. She's broken, Loxley dear. All broken inside. All she needs is your prayers," Aunt Dot answered in a wooden voice as she carried our nearly full plates to the kitchen and began tidying up from supper. She didn't seem to notice that I barely touched my food or that she'd eaten even less. "Your presence wouldn't do anything but confuse her." Of course, I had no argument for that.

I helped Aunt Dot with the chores, but I moped the entire time. Why couldn't she understand that I wanted to talk about Momma? I needed to because a strange sort of thing was happening to me. A very strange thing. I didn't want to acknowledge it, but the fear of it grew bigger every day. One day, I would end up in an asylum just like Momma. *Please, Daddy, don't let that be true.* But what if I was like her? What could be done? What if one day I would go crazy too? I thought perhaps I would. The kids at school believed it well enough.

All those Belle girls are crazy. The whole family needs to be committed or put down.

Shannon Bohannan didn't care that my locker was only two down from hers. She didn't care that I could hear every word she said, and Shannon said the most awful things. She *wanted* me to hear her. She made her thoughts known to whoever would listen, and that was everyone because she was the most popular girl in school. Everywhere she went, a flock of girls followed, and the boys were never too far behind. This afternoon's diatribe had been the worst yet, and nobody seemed to mind that her cruel tongue often brought me to tears.

"It doesn't matter how much money you have if you're crazy, Betty Lou. Money can't buy happiness or love—or sanity. Nobody wants to go to prom with a mental case. I bet she won't even have a date. It's probably for the best. We don't want to have any episodes at our dance, do we?" My schoolmates agreed with a flurry of giggles and a few not-so-soft whispers. All derogatory. Even Louise Walcott turned her back on me. Once upon a time, we had been friends.

Shannon rolled her eyes at me now and twisted her long ponytail with her finger before tossing it over her shoulder. The other girls were gathered so tightly around her that I was surprised she could take a step without tripping over one of them. Before leaving, she tilted her haughty head as if she smelled something bad. Presumably me. The rest of her flock followed suit.

Nobody noticed that her gold charm bracelet hit the ground.

None of her so-called friends asked her about it as they prissed away. Shannon Bohannan's charm bracelet, the one that she'd spent all lunch period showing off to everyone, lay on the floor before me like a golden siren. I saw it and without thinking one extra second picked it up and dropped it in my jacket pocket. Nobody had seen me. I was pretty sure of that. There was no one in the hallway except one boy, a new boy, Harmon. He smiled at me, closed his locker and walked away. He had a pleasant enough smile, but it was a bit too big for his face. It made me shiver. Could he have seen me claim Shannon's lost treasure? No, he hadn't, and it was mine now. I felt powerful and a bit darker as I closed my locker and hurried off to class with no one the wiser.

The rest of the day had seemed like a dream. Aunt Dot allowed me to drive the car to school on Fridays, in case I wanted to go to the ice cream shop. I never went, but she was always hopeful that I would one day. Poor Aunt Dot. I must truly be a disappointment to her. I'd parked the car down by the river and made the walk to Summerleigh.

And now I was leaving, although I would have loved nothing more than to walk the grounds or explore Jeopardy's castle room. I'd hidden one of my treasure boxes in the attic, but I couldn't linger today. Aunt Dot would be expecting me home. She was determined to take me dress shopping for the school's end-of-year dance. And I could think of nothing I wanted to do less. At least she would be present as a chaperone; her being there would likely shut the mouths of the girls who expressed their raw hatred of me so vociferously.

Goodbye, Summerleigh. I will be back soon. Keep my treasures safe!

And as if it heard me and agreed, the house groaned a little.

As I made the sweaty walk back to the car, I began to experience feelings of impending doom. Weighty emotions like grief and sorrow struck me, and by the time I arrived back to the car and put the keys in the ignition, I was in tears. The only consolation was that Daddy had suddenly joined me. His presence, prized and precious to me, also disturbed me greatly now. He'd never left Summerleigh before. He always pottered around with his plants and pots when he wasn't walking the halls making sure the place was safe. But then as suddenly as he appeared, he disappeared, as if he knew his presence caused me to worry. I managed to brush away the tears before turning onto Highway 98, but I prayed all the way home.

When I arrived, I spotted Reverend Bartlett's car in the driveway and realized that all the praying in the world wasn't going to reverse whatever doom awaited me. Had the school called? Was I going to jail for my heinous deeds? Had my thieving ways finally caught up to me? Certainly, they would have called the sheriff out here, not the pastor.

Oh, Daddy, please stay with me. Don't leave me now.

No manner of pleading would compel him to come with me, and I walked inside alone.

Chapter One—Jerica

"You two go have fun and don't give us a second thought. Jordan and I will have a grand old time without you two cramping our style. Jordan loves his Aunt Ree-Ree. Don't you, sugar?" Renee kissed my son's cheeks, and he laughed with delight. Yes, he did love her, and she'd been in his life from day one. I was grateful for her help since my parents were gone and I had no siblings. Mommyhood was a scary job.

"Thanks, Aunt Ree-Ree. You two don't get too wild. We won't be gone long," I promised as I did my best to put on a happy face. Wow, new mommy guilt was a real thing.

"Are you two sure this is how you want to spend your day off together? Working in a dirty old shed? Honestly, I've never seen two goofier people. Getting all worked up about carpentry. Mommy and Daddy are crazy, Jordan. I'd rather be at the beach, wouldn't you?" Jesse and I grinned at each other. We *were* goofy, and I didn't take Renee's opinion as criticism. She just had no filter, and I had no doubt she thought we were an odd couple. "I guess everyone has to have a hobby. That must be the secret to a good relationship. You need to have a mutual hobby. Maybe Frank and I should take up something together. But what? I love bingo. What do you think, Jordan? Should Aunt Ree-Ree take Uncle Frank to bingo?"

Jesse laughed at that. "You are never going to get Frank anywhere near a bingo hall. I hate to say it, but he is probably the unluckiest guy I've ever met. But at least he has you, so maybe that means his luck is turning." He hugged her neck and kissed Jordan's plump cheek. It was hard to believe that our little one was three months old today. Until now, except for one dinner date, I had made it a point not to be too far from him for very long. I liked being at home and witnessing all of his firsts. But let's face it, at three months old, there weren't a lot of significant firsts going on except some cooing and turning over. It was a good thing I had quick reflexes, or else Jordan would've hit the floor this morning. I'd only turned my back for a few seconds, but that was long enough for him to navigate the diaper changing table and almost roll onto the floor. I cried for fifteen minutes, which made him cry, and we were both two blubber boxes by the time Jesse came home from the grocery store. I had not confessed that horrible near accident to anyone, not even Jesse, but Jordan knew. And so did I.

Man, I'm not too good at this, but I love you, Jordan.

Jesse's cousin Renee was a reliable person, and I didn't believe she'd ever make such a horrible mistake. She would never take her eyes off a curious baby. I had no worries about that. Renee had no children of her own, but it wasn't too late. Her plumbing worked fine, as she often reminded me. And with her and Frisky Frank, as Jesse and I secretly called him, anything was possible.

"Go, Jerica. Before you change your mind. You've got some remodeling to do. I'll have lunch ready when you two get back. See you around noontime. Shoo!"

"Sounds great," Jesse said as he tugged on my shirt sleeve.

I waved goodbye to Jordan, who had no idea what was going on except that funny Aunt Ree-Ree was playing games with him. I guess it was a good thing that he was focused on Renee's comical face. Here lately, he cried whenever I left his line of sight. The door closed behind us, and Jesse and I stepped out into the sunshine. It was a beautiful day at Summerleigh, and it felt good to go outside and stretch my bones. There were things that needed to be tended to around here, but this new find had captured our attention.

"You got everything you need?" I asked Jesse as we loaded up into his truck.

"Yeah, I think so. I just hope that pothole hasn't grown any bigger, but I can navigate around it. Definitely got to take care of this road, though. At least the rain stopped." Jesse was right to worry about the condition of the dirt roads that trailed around our house. It had been raining for days. I didn't realize how dreary the gray skies had left me feeling.

"Any idea what this place was? I mean, it's so far away from the river that it couldn't have been used for a fishing shack. Could it?"

"A playhouse, maybe, or another potting shed. The possibilities are endless, but I know what it's going to be." Jesse didn't seem too concerned with the origins of the shed, but I had a nagging curiosity.

"It's too well-built to be a potting shed—and too large. But whatever it was, I'm glad we're doing this. This was a great idea of mine, wasn't it?" I smiled at him flirtatiously.

It was true that it had been my idea to transform this old shack or shed or whatever it was into Jesse's own space. When I suggested it, I didn't realize that we'd be doing the remodeling right this week. It had been so long since I worked a sander or held a saw. True, we had plenty of room at Summerleigh for a writer's den, especially when we were experiencing a seasonal downturn in our bed-and-breakfast's business, but this place was meant for something special. I could just feel it. And Jesse deserved a place of his own, a place to get lost in his stories, his own little spot where he could go write himself into a frenzy. I wanted that for him. It had been a long time since he'd written anything, and he needed to get back into the swing of things. That's what he needed. We had both immersed ourselves in our new lives as parents and business owners and the sometimes-challenging aspects of learning about one another. My husband loved Jordan and me, but Jesse Clarke needed to write the next book. For him. And I knew for a fact he had plenty of stories to tell. He'd given the Belles life with his last book and very respectfully shared their tragic tales with the world, but now it was time to move on and do something fresh and new.

"It's a great idea. I've never had a writer's shack before. It is away from the house, though. What if you need me?"

"I know how to pick up a phone, Jess. Or we can install one of those fancy intercoms." His eyes widened, and he cocked his head to the side. "I'm just joking. The whole point of you going to your shack—excuse me, your writer's den—is to get lost in the words, right? You don't need any interruptions. I'll be okay. Oh, there it is. I can't believe this was here the whole time and we never knew it. It makes you wonder what else is on this property."

"I wouldn't be surprised if there is more to see. The more woods we clear, the more we tidy the place up, the more I am amazed by it all. I wish there was a way I could thank Harper. Her gift to you changed both of our lives."

I squeezed his hand. "She knows. I think she visits once in a while." I didn't dwell on that statement. Jesse was happy believing the Belle family was happy and at rest. I guessed I believed that too, but sometimes...

"It is possible that John Jeffrey Belle built it. Or maybe old Ben Hartley. He did a lot of work around the place before he went...before he got sick." We came to a stop in front of the small wooden building. It had one window on the front—a small window that was dirty and would need replacing. There were a slender door and a very small porch too. There were two windows on either side of the structure but none at the back. Jesse turned off the engine, and I grabbed my work gloves from the glove box.

Yep, it was going to be great getting all dirty. I still couldn't believe that we hadn't known this building even existed a week ago. I smiled at him as we headed toward the shed. It really was a well-built building.

"I'd say maybe eighty years old, maybe ninety." Jesse rubbed the wood with his fingers and studied the woodwork like the professional carpenter he was, and I agreed with him.

"Maybe older. Who knows?" The front door opened easily despite its age and bad condition. We stepped inside, and I immediately felt as if I had stepped back in time. Yeah, this place was like a time capsule. The dated furniture would have to go, and that made me sad. None of it was really valuable, but a small part of me wanted to keep it. I loved old things, and so did my husband. Between the two of us, we could very easily become hoarders, but thankfully we had Renee in our lives. She always brought us back down to earth.

"I guess we ought to get started. Shouldn't take us long to get all the stuff out here. I'm anxious to take a look at the wood. You think the floors are okay?" I asked as I reached for the nearest broken chair.

Jesse slid his gloves on and then halfheartedly jumped up and down. With a grin, he said, "It feels promising, not spongy, but we'll have to see if that's true for the whole room. I'm hoping. Let's get this loaded." And that's what we did for the next hour. We dragged out dusty furniture and boxes of junk. There was nothing of worth in any of the boxes, but there was plenty of evidence that rodents had regularly visited the place. I kept my eye out for snakes and rats. Unfortunately for Jesse, I insisted on going through every single box before committing it to the junk pile. As soon as we got the last box out, we attempted to move the only table in the room. It was surprisingly heavy, and I couldn't for the life of me figure out how we were going to get it through the door. It didn't break into parts or come apart. It appeared that whoever brought the desk in here had actually built it in this room, which seemed a strange thing.

"Ugh, what are you going to do? I'm not strong enough to carry this monstrosity too far. And there's the question of how to break it down."

Jesse rubbed his hand across the surface of the table. "You know, I might just keep it. Maybe it was meant to be here. Kind of feels like that. I'd need to sand it and maybe paint it, but I'll make it work."

"Paint it? The heck you say. Let's sweep this floor and look at the wood." I headed to Jesse's truck and grabbed the brooms. The floor was so covered in grime that it would take forever to get it clean, but we were anxious to really have a good look at her bones. As my dad used to say, if you have a good floor, that's a great place to start. Together we manned the brooms and got the dirt out in about thirty minutes. We moved enough of it that we finally got a decent look at the amazing wooden floor that lay hidden beneath.

"This is great! I don't see any damage at all. This is going to be an amazing place when we're finished with it, Jerica. Thank you." We were covered in dirt and still holding our brooms, dust particles floating around us, but Jesse squeezed me up in his arms and I didn't struggle. It'd been a while since we'd been "alone together," and it was nice to flirt again. Or rather it was nice to flirt with the potential of it going somewhere other than a kiss on the cheek and a sleepy good night. I felt tired a lot since Jordan came. I couldn't explain why, other than that I dreamed about Marisol all the time. Sometimes at night when I paced the floor with my colicky baby, I imagined I saw a little shadow sneaking around corners, moving past me in the hall. But it had only been hopeful imaginings. My mind didn't really want her to come back, but my heart missed her with all my being.

Marisol, you should see your little brother. You would love him.

I lost myself in Jesse's affection, praying that the grief would pass and I could enjoy the moment.

No, Jerica. Don't do this. You released her when you laid Jeopardy to rest. Don't summon her back.

"Jerica," Jesse whispered in my ear, "I love you." The air in the room felt lighter, the lingering grief vanished, and I welcomed his embrace. *We're alone; may as well make the most of the moment. Nobody would know.* As if we were both thinking the same thing, we dropped our brooms. Jesse caught me up in his arms and kissed me passionately, and I met it with my own need. Next thing I knew, we were against the wall, still kissing, and then he carried me to the table without missing a beat. Luckily, boxes had been stacked on top of the table and the top wasn't too dirty. Our hands were everywhere, my skin was sweaty, and it wasn't even ten o'clock yet.

Were we really going to do this here? It felt so wild, and I wasn't one to do wild things. Not really.

Suddenly, Jesse paused and said, "What is that?"

Confused and a little disappointed, I stopped and turned to look behind me. There were scratch marks on the table. No, not scratch marks but words. Jesse released me gently and I rearranged my top as both of us peered at what appeared to be words carved into the wood panel. If it had been just a name or some initials, I wouldn't have thought it much to look at, but it was more than that.

Carved sloppily, in all capital letters, was a name I knew but hadn't seen or heard in a very long time. Except in my own mind. I rubbed the carving with my fingers but shuddered at the rest of the phrase. The long, exaggerated strike marks filled me with dread. All the warmth left the shack, and I withdrew my hand.

YOU'RE MINE, LOXLEY.

Chapter Two—Loxley

When I arrived home, I found Aunt Dot in the living room weeping on Reverend Bartlett's bony shoulder. Her red nose, damp eyes and runny mascara were additional clues that all was not well. A tragedy of some sort must have occurred because Aunt Dot didn't cry at the drop of a hat. The presence of the pastor disturbed me no end.

"No," I whispered as my aunt approached me. "No, please, Aunt Dot. Don't say it."

Her tiny frame vibrated with grief as she rose from the couch. Her small mouth worked, but nothing came out except a sob. Her face was in her hands as Reverend Bartlett remembered himself. He placed an awkward arm around her sagging shoulders.

"There now, Dorothy. You did all you could for her. You have to think of the child now."

What child was he referring to? Me?

And then I knew. I knew it all, but my intuition offered me no comfort. Momma was dead—not Harper or Addison. At least there was that. But Momma was gone forever! I would never see her again. Not on this side of heaven, if either of us made it there. For the first time in my entire life, I felt real anger toward Aunt Dot. It was real and vicious, and it bubbled up inside me from somewhere dark and dangerous.

"I knew she needed me! I knew it, and you wouldn't let me go. I should have visited her, Aunt Dot. Why didn't you let me go? I'll never see Momma again, will I? That's it, isn't it? If we had gone to see her, none of this would have happened!" It was a ridiculous thing to say, and I didn't even understand why I would say such a thing, but the words flew out of my mouth like bats out of hell. Better than screaming my head off and expressing all the anger that filled my soul. But I needed to scream! Scream to the heavens as loudly as I could. Didn't God see anything that was going on down here?

Reverend Bartlett stuttered as he tried to take command of the situation. "Now, young lady. Don't say things you will regret later. Especially to your sweet aunt. After all she's done for you, Loxley, you and your sisters should be eternally grateful. She didn't have to take you in, but she did out of the goodness of her heart. You may have lost a mother, but she lost a sister. Your Momma was a very unbalanced woman."

Not unlike you, I imagined him thinking. He was a pastor, so he probably knew all my secrets. Didn't God tell pastors secrets? That proved it; if Momma was crazy, then I must be too. Those things were inherited. I read that in a magazine once, one of Dr. Earl's magazines he left out in his waiting room. I put my hands to my ears, as if I could make it all go away by stopping the noise of my own mind. Aunt Dot continued to weep; she sagged now and collapsed on the sofa.

I fled the living room and slammed my bedroom door as hard as I could. I wanted to shut him out! I knew Momma was crazy—I knew better than he did. Who was he to judge me? I turned on my small bedside radio. Perry Como sang *No Other Love* as I emptied my soul of every available tear. I cried so hard

I thought I might throw up, but after lying on my bed for what felt like an eternity, I fell asleep.

When I woke up, the radio had been turned off and it was dark out. The door to my room was ajar. Light from the hallway shone on my face, and I realized there was a figure sitting beside me. Tall, with excellent posture. Too tall to be Aunt Dot. "Momma?" I whispered as I tried to sit up without scaring her away.

"No. It's me, Loxley Grace. Harper." She clicked on my pink lamp, and I could see her face clearly. I threw my arms around her neck, and together we cried for Momma. "I know, I know."

"I wanted to see Momma, Harper. I knew I needed to go. Now I'll never know…" I sobbed as she held me a little while longer.

"Know what, Loxley?"

I pulled away from her and clutched my favorite teddy bear. I'd almost let my secret slip, but I couldn't do that. If I told Harper my fears, that I not only saw ghosts but heard people's thoughts and did the most horrible things, she would hate me. Just like she hated Momma. I couldn't stand it if she hated me.

"Tell me, Loxley Belle. Know what?"

I stared into the face of my teddy bear. The toy's black glass eyes did not judge me. They didn't see anything. I clutched it tightly to my chest as I leaned back on my sagging pillow. It was ridiculous for a girl my age to still have teddy bears and dolls, but I couldn't let them go. They had been my friends for such a long time, and once in a while, the Ghost Boy came to touch them. But he never stayed long because he belonged at Summerleigh, just like I did.

"What happened to Momma, Harper?"

"Aunt Dot didn't say exactly, but she had been sick for a long time. Momma had a weak heart." *Oh, no. She died of a broken heart.* "None of what happened to Momma or Daddy or even Jeopardy is your fault. None of it, Loxley Belle," she said as she patted my leg. I sobbed some more, and we comforted one another, but she gave up trying to cajole me into telling her what I was talking about.

Harper went to my closet and began sliding my clothes around. "What are you doing?"

"You need a black dress for the funeral. I don't see a single black thing in here, but that's understandable. We'll have to rectify that, sister."

"I don't want to go to her funeral," I said as I turned my radio back on. Strangely enough, it was Perry Como again, only this time he was singing *Don't Let the Stars Get in Your Eyes*. I didn't turn it up loud, but it was loud enough to discourage further conversation. I wanted to sulk—I needed to sulk. For how long? I couldn't say.

"You have to attend Momma's funeral, but I'll be with you every step of the way. Don't worry about the dress. I have to go shopping, anyway. I'll pick one up for you. You seem taller, though, a bit more slender." She ignored my diversion tactic and continued to politely search through my closet. "Shoes too. Still a size seven shoe?"

I nodded my answer. Harper closed the closet door and sat on the side of my bed again. I wanted to be mad at her too, so mad that I could ignore her reasonable demeanor, but it was impossible. "I love you, Loxley. So does Aunt Dot. You have a lot of feelings bubbling up inside of you. I understand that. Remember when Daddy died? I thought I would never get over it. And then Jeopardy…"

We sat in silence for a little while as Perry sang to us. "It will get better, I promise. You probably have a lot of good memories of Momma—hold on to them. Treasure them. Think about them. I am going to do the same thing. We will cry a lot, and we will be angry, but it's important that we don't turn our anger on the wrong person. None of this is fair, Loxley. None of it."

I felt Harper's hand tremble, and her eyes blinked erratically, but it only lasted a few seconds. Yes, this was hard on her too. I was being selfish. Completely selfish.

"I love you, Harper."

"I love you too, Loxley. You know Aunt Dot loves you to smithereens. You are her whole world. Don't be unkind to her."

"I don't mean to be, but I tried to tell her that I wanted to see Momma. You don't understand, Harper. You just don't understand." I gripped my teddy bear tight and closed my eyes. My sister said nothing, but I continued to feel her quiver ever so slightly. When she clutched my hand, I opened my eyes.

Harper's face conveyed her hurt, but she didn't snap at me. "I'll be back tomorrow afternoon. I'm going to see Addison now and will do the shopping in the morning. The funeral is the day after tomorrow."

"You aren't staying here with us?"

"Not tonight. I'll come stay tomorrow, though. Are you willing to share a bed with me, little sister?"

I squeezed her hand as she rose from the bed and smiled down at me. Yes, she looked so much like Momma. So much that it broke my heart. "Please remember what I said. Be kind to Aunt Dot." And then she left me alone with my teddy bear and my thoughts. Eventually, I got up and went to the restroom to wash my face and put on my pajamas. I wasn't hungry even though it was well past supper time. As I stepped out of the bathroom, I heard Aunt Dot crying. She wept soft and mournful tears—the sound of it nearly broke my heart. She was in her room with the door shut, and she was obviously making an effort to keep me from hearing her.

Terrible shame enveloped me. Harper was right, but then again, she usually was right. About everything. I should never have been so unkind to Aunt Dot. I walked to her door and poised my hand to knock. That's when I realized my mistake. Aunt Dot wasn't crying; it was someone else. And the crying wasn't coming from her room but mine. As I turned my head, I could see a figure standing at the far end of the hall. The kitchen light fell behind her, and I could make out a petite silhouette. *Aunt Dot!* But if Aunt Dot wasn't in my room weeping her heart out and Harper was gone, who was in my bedroom? As the sobs continued, I knew. No, I hadn't heard her voice in a very long time, but I would never forget it. Never.

Momma was here, and she was crying. Crying for me, crying because I had let her down. If I had come, if I had visited her, it would have cheered her right up. She would have known that I loved her, that I had always loved her. Aunt Dot joined me outside my room. I moved toward the door, but she gripped my elbow gently and shook her head. With a finger to her lips, she stepped in front of me and opened the door quickly.

There was no one there. No one at all. Momma had been here, though. She had been here, and now she was gone. And my teddy bear had been moved. It was sitting in my rocking chair with my rose pink blanket tucked around it. Aunt Dot walked to the radio, but I had not left it on. My window was open slightly because it was a warm night, but there was no sound from outdoors that could have seeped inside. It was late, and our neighborhood was quiet except for a dog barking in the distance. Aunt Dot glanced at me, her eyes fearful. She closed the door, took me by the hand and led me to her room.

We didn't talk, but I hugged her and we waited to hear Momma again. But she never made another sound. Sometime near sunup, I fell asleep. I woke up confused as to how I ended up in Aunt Dot's bed, but then the memory of last night's visitation came back to me in a rush. I sat upright in the bed, my eyes sticky, my body tired. I had missed my opportunity to talk to Momma, but I was pretty sure I knew where I could find her. And I would not be denied.

I had to go to Summerleigh. Momma couldn't or wouldn't stay here. Not as long as Aunt Dot was around. That had to have been why she didn't return last night. I had been afraid at first, fearful at hearing her crying. But now that the shock had worn off, I wanted to hear her again more than anything.

And I could. But I had to get to Summerleigh first.

Chapter Three—Jerica

It was morning, and the sun poured in through the big window over the sink. I stared at the gardens as I washed the serving tray. Jordan cooed happily in his baby seat on the floor just a few feet away from me. He was just about too heavy to lift now. Which was fine with him because he preferred my arms to his carrier, crib or swing. Not so fine for my back, which seemed to ache quite a bit lately. That was part of the reason why I begged off on helping Jesse with working on his writer's shack. That and it was too hot out for Jordan. He didn't like to be hot and much preferred wearing nothing but a diaper. But I couldn't let my back and Jordan's fussy mood distract me; we had a large party of vacationers coming in at the end of the week, which was great because the till was getting low. We were comfortable, for now, but with a son to raise and diapers to buy, we needed to keep our eye on the bottom line.

Jordan blew bubbles and cooed at the toy that hung over his carrier. "What's that, Jordie? You see the giraffe?" That excited him even more. He got his arms and legs moving, kicking away in excitement. Thank goodness he was happy today. "I love you, Momma's boy." He smiled at me and went back to focusing on the rattling toy. The more he moved, the more it rattled. This was the perfect gizmo for keeping an active baby entertained for a few minutes. Just a few more minutes, though, because naptime was quickly approaching. If I was lucky, I would get all my wisteria plates washed and dried. *Oof! I'd gotten this water a little too hot.* I smiled at Jordan again as I turned my attention back to the wide backyard. It was such a beautiful day. Just glorious. I thought about Jesse and how he was progressing, but I wasn't going to call him. I meant what I said about not calling him while he was in his shack. *Hmm...maybe after his nap, Jordan will tolerate a car ride.*

A sliding sound shook me out of my reverie.

What in the world could that be? My hands still in the water, I glanced around and was surprised to see that Jordan's carrier had moved about two feet. He wasn't crying, but he wasn't playing with his toy. He stared at me as if to say, "What did you do that for?" I snatched my hands out of the water and dried them as I squatted down in front of him.

"Hey, how did you do that?" I asked nervously as I patted around the carrier. There was nothing on the floor, no water, nothing slick that would account for the carrier shifting or moving. Just as I was thinking that this wasn't safe, the carrier moved again. Only it slid back and away from me as if an invisible force were taking my child away from me.

"Stop!" I yelled, and then Jordan began to cry. I gripped the carrier and unbuckled my son with shaking hands. I lifted him from the carrier and backpedaled away from the thing.

"Whoever or whatever you are, that's not acceptable. You leave my son alone, you hear me!" I shouted as Jordan wailed along with me. "It's okay, baby. It's okay." I reached for the car keys but thought better of it. I couldn't drive without putting him back in the carrier. That wasn't an option.

"It's okay, Jordie. Everything is alright now." The phone rang, and I snatched it up awkwardly. "Hello?"

"Hey." Jesse's voice on the phone was like a voice from heaven. "Sounds like Jordan is having a bad afternoon. I've gotten quite a bit done here. Do I need to come back to the house?"

"He's...the baby seat just moved, and we're a little freaked out. Yes! Please come...I don't know. Would you mind coming back for a few minutes?"

"I'm on the way. Let me shut this saw down and get the cords inside. I'll be there in two minutes."

"Okay," I said as I breathed a sigh of relief. I took a still-crying Jordan out the back door and paced as I waited for Jesse on the porch. "It's okay, Jordie. It's okay. I didn't mean to scare you." His lips crinkled up, and he had big glassy tears in his eyes. I kissed his forehead and got a good whiff of him. "No wonder you're crying," I said, smiling at him like there was nothing wrong. "You smell. You're a smelly little booger." His tears dried up soon, but I would certainly have to tidy him up before his nap. By the time Jesse got back to Summerleigh, Jordan was fussy but not crying. The truck rolled to a stop, and I just blurted it all out. Jesse hurried inside with me to take a look at the carrier.

"You aren't hurt, are you? How's Jordan? Oh, never mind. I can smell him a mile away."

"Yes, he's about to get a nap, but look at this. The carrier was here right next to me at the sink, and then I...I heard it move. You know, like a sliding sound. When I went to check it out, the thing moved like six feet."

"You're kidding." Jesse took off his tool belt and laid it on the nearby table. He checked out the floor, but there wasn't any evidence that the carrier had been dragged or moved. "I can't see how that could happen."

"Nevertheless, it did," I said as I shifted the baby to my other arm. He weighed a ton, and he wasn't happy with me at all.

"Could you have been mistaken? Bumped it, maybe?"

"I swear it happened just like I said. I was nowhere near it. I could see him right there, just a few feet away."

Jesse rubbed his chin thoughtfully. "Maybe you splashed some water on the floor?"

"Really, Sherlock? When I looked back, he was a few feet over. Then the carrier moved again, right in front of me. I mean, I was looking directly at the dang thing."

Jesse shook his head, and sawdust from his hair floated around him. "I'm not doubting you, Jerica. I believe it happened. I'm just looking at all the possibilities as to why it happened. The floor looks level. How long did this last?"

What a dumb, unimportant question.

I was quickly losing my temper. "I don't know. A few seconds. Long enough for me to be freaked out over it, and Jordan..." The baby started crying again, and who could blame him? He had a smelly diaper and parents who were on the verge of having a serious argument. "You know what? I'll just go change our son while you play Nancy Drew. Say what you want, I saw the damn thing move."

"I never doubted you. Why are you so hostile?"

I raised my hand to let him know I wasn't in the mood for his theories. "Never mind. Thanks for nothing," I said as I stormed out of the kitchen, through the parlor and up the stairs. Imagine not believing me. What a jerk. What a complete... As I climbed each step, I felt my anger waning. By the time I made it to the landing, I was wondering what just happened. Just a few seconds ago, I wanted to pinch my husband's head off. Now I was wishing he were up here with me.

But I knew for a fact that baby carrier moved.

"I'm not sure what happened, Jordan, but I'm going to stay with you. I promise. I'm not going to take my eyes off you." True to my word, I kept my eyes on him the whole time while I changed his diaper and struggled with him to change his t-shirt. He had his lunch all over his shirt. Darn it, I had stomped off without bringing his bottle with me, and he was going to need it. Jordan Clarke was a bottle baby, for sure.

Jesse must have read my mind because he appeared with the bottle and the baby carrier. I shook my head. "I don't want that in here if you don't mind." He shrugged and put the carrier in the hallway. Jordan saw his dad and reached his chubby hand out for him. His eyes were getting redder by the second.

"You're down for the count now, aren't you, buddy?" Jesse came up behind me and put his arms around my waist. The baby smiled and then closed his eyes and drank his sleepy self into a stupor. "I'm sorry, Jerica. I really don't doubt you. I thought I was comforting you."

"No, I'm sorry. I flew off the handle for no reason."

Jesse kissed my neck. "I should have stayed home today and helped out. You didn't sleep well last night, or the night before that. You're probably exhausted." He kissed my cheek now, but I artfully removed myself from his arms. I knew where this was going, and I wasn't quite ready to get cozy. Our son's baby carrier just slid across the room.

"You think I hallucinated the carrier moving because I was tired?" I shook my head but remembered to keep my voice down so as not to wake up the baby.

"No, I'm not talking about the carrier. I'm talking about you. Let me put him down for his nap, and you go do something just for you. Take a hot shower, read a book. I'm done for the day." He slid his arms under the baby, and I gave him up without a struggle. My back was killing me now.

"I want Hannah to come, Jesse. To Summerleigh. I need her to see if there's anything here. Can you call Renee? Hannah's cell phone isn't working, or the number's been changed...or something," I said, embarrassed by my confession. Yes, I had called Hannah. She was an amazing and gifted sensitive. If anyone could figure out what was here at Summerleigh, it would be her.

"If it makes you happy, I'll do it, but I think you might be jumping the gun a little," he said as he put the baby in his crib.

That hot shower idea sounded terrific, and I wasn't in the mood to argue anymore. But I wasn't changing my mind on this either. "Maybe so, but better to be safe than sorry. Right?"

I could see his shoulders sag a little as he nodded. I'd won this battle, but I didn't feel good about it. Who would? I thought all the Belles would be at rest. I thought they would be settled and resting in peace. Who else would be here? A member of the McIntyre family? I didn't believe that, not after finding that threat carved in the desk.

You're mine, Loxley.

I walked down the hall and popped into my bedroom to grab my robe. I let the shower get nice and steamy before stepping in. Gosh, my back ached. What had I done to myself?

Just as I was beginning to shed my clothes, I froze. In the foggy mirror, I saw a face. A familiar face. Not the girl with the braids, but she had the same eyes. Those same *I-can-see-things-you-can't*, faraway eyes.

I was looking at the face of Loxley Belle.

Chapter Four—Loxley

We all looked like a bunch of black crows hovering around Momma's graveside. None of us would have been stylish enough for Momma's taste, except maybe Augustine Hogue, who'd remarkably lost quite a bit of weight in recent years and was as slim and fit as Momma ever had been. I felt sure that Momma would not like to have been one-upped at her own funeral. But then again, there had been no viewing of her. Did she even know we were here? Since that one time when I heard her crying at Aunt Dot's, I hadn't heard her again or seen her. And the place had been so busy. Suddenly, we had plenty of friends who came to mourn with us. There had been no time to slip away and make the drive to Summerleigh, although I was just as determined to go as I had been.

Reverend Bartlett did a masterful job of describing heaven and how we could all get there, but there was not even a hint of a promise that Ann Marie Belle had made it through the pearly gates.

Silly girl. You know Momma isn't going to make it to heaven. You know that. Neither are you if you continue sneaking and stealing. You're just a big ol' sinner, Loxley Grace Belle. And that preacher knows it—everyone here knows it.

The voice in my head was my own, but I believed it. My hand patted inside the pocket of my fitted blazer. I could feel the pen, cold, hard evidence of my latest crime. I couldn't help myself. The pen was black and shiny and had a feather on the cap. I'd had to take the cap off to fit the pen in my pocket. I was sure it was leaking ink inside my jacket, but that hadn't stopped me from taking it. It was quite fancy and nothing like anything I owned. It was only a memento, nothing terribly expensive like a charm bracelet. This was just something to remember Momma by, and it was not like I had planned to take anything. The minister glanced at me as he paused to catch his breath. No doubt he'd yammer on for a while longer. He had a captive audience here at the First Baptist Church of Desire's cemetery. The seat beside me was empty; that was Addison's spot. Wouldn't you know the morning we buried Momma, Addison decided to go have that baby? What a terrible day to be born. To be born on the day of your grandmother's funeral...that child was sure to be as haunted as me.

I peeked at Harper, who rubbed at her bloodshot eyes with a handkerchief. There were real tears there; I don't know why that surprised me. Aunt Dot sat beside her, the two of them holding hands, but I kept my hands in my lap. I didn't want to hold anyone's hand or be comforted in any kind of way. The longer I pretended none of this was happening, the longer I could avoid the inevitable truth. Ann Marie Belle was alive somewhere, surely. Why else weren't we allowed to see her? But that couldn't be right because I heard Momma crying. This all seemed so surreal, like a bad dream. Momma just couldn't be lying in that powder blue casket. Surely, she'd done something shameful to herself. I had the sneaking suspicion that that was the case indeed. What had she done to herself? Why wouldn't anyone tell me? I'd read the obituary, but it offered me no clues, no evidence of Momma's death. It's like she was never really here…except she was because I was here, and Harper was here too. And then, just like that, we were being asked to approach the casket. Someone handed each of us a white rose and prompted us to place them on the casket. I didn't want to give the rose away. What was Momma going to do with these flowers? She was stuffed in the casket and never coming out. *Why can't I see her?*

And then the weight of the world felt as if it landed on my shoulders. Right square on my shoulders. All my sorrow bubbled out of me, and I clutched the flower so hard a forgotten thorn stabbed me. I placed the flower on top of the casket as Harper directed me to, and I felt my sister's arms around me. I buried my face in her coat and cried. Harper didn't cry now; she let me do all the crying as she whispered, "I love you, Loxley." After a few minutes, Aunt Dot led us both to the waiting car. It was a big black sedan, not the convertible we usually drove around town in. I was glad we weren't in the convertible today. I didn't want to be seen, and I'd had enough of sympathetic family friends. Through blurry eyes, I could see lines of cars hugging the curb. I'd never seen so many cars, except at our high school football games. Everyone came out for those. I would never have guessed that so many people remembered her. I guess the Daughdrill name still had some pull in our county. Surely, they weren't here for us. Folks from everywhere had come to pay their respects to Momma. It was an amazing sight considering she didn't really have any friends. None of us Belles did except one another. These weren't our friends either, just looky-loos who came to see if Momma was truly dead. If the mad, beautiful Ann Marie Belle had finally succumbed to her own madness. I could almost hear them whispering now, just like the girls at school, whispering away.

"Loxley, let's go home, dearest," Aunt Dot said softly, and I obeyed her without argument. The ride home was long, and I laid my head in Harper's lap. With loving hands, she swept my hair out of my face. Her hands weren't cool like Momma's had been, but at least she loved me. "One of us needs to go to the hospital, Harper. People will want to come by the house, though, mostly the ladies from the church who insist on dropping off food. I don't want to leave Loxley alone."

I didn't like that my aunt talked about me as if I were a child, as if I weren't there at all, but I didn't have the energy to protest her proposal. I couldn't shake the image of Momma's coffin being lowered into that dark pit. I didn't actually see that, but I knew it would happen as soon as we left the graveside.

"I'll stay with Loxley, Aunt Dot. You go be with Addison. You're right that someone should be there to welcome the baby," Harper said as she continued to stroke my hair.

"Thank you," Aunt Dot answered as she pressed her twisted hankie to her nose and stared out the window. It had begun to rain, and the sky was as gray as any I'd seen. The car dropped us off at our aunt's home and drove away. To my surprise and relief, there was no one there to meet us. No helpful neighbors with armloads of groceries or piping-hot casseroles. Not that I could stand to eat anything. Aunt Dot was delusional if she thought anyone cared about us. Nobody cared. Nobody loved us Belles. I shoved the key in the door, and we hurried inside to avoid getting soaked through. "I'll make us some supper," Harper offered. "Why don't you make us both a glass of iced tea? I'd like lemon in mine, if you have it."

"We don't have any lemon, and I don't want any supper, Harper," I said as she ignored me.

"You never could say no to my buttermilk biscuits." She smiled knowingly and began ransacking the cabinets for the ingredients. She was right, of course; I couldn't say no to Harper's biscuits. "Do you have any peaches?" We always had peaches when we lived at Summerleigh. It was a wonder we weren't pure-dee sick of them. Harper usually put them up, but she always allowed me to add just a touch of cinnamon.

"I think so. Aunt Dot and I put a few jars up last year."

"Only a few?" Harper asked as she reached for the glass bowl and heated up the oven.

"Yes, just a few she got from the produce stand in town. I told her there were oodles of peaches at Summerleigh, but she wouldn't let me go pick them. Imagine all those peaches falling to the ground, just rotting away with no one to eat them. Momma would have a fit if she knew about it. How many times do you suppose we climbed those trees, Harper?"

"More times than I care to remember. Do you remember when Jeopardy chased that cat up the big peach tree?"

And so the conversation went for a while. By the time Harper made the biscuits and set the cast-iron skillet in the oven, my stomach was rumbling with hunger. My grief had not dissipated, not in the least, but I felt comforted by Harper's presence and the promise of buttermilk biscuits. Of course, I was painfully aware that she wouldn't be here long. Just a few more days, if that. And then I would be alone with Aunt Dot. I only ever saw Addison occasionally, and that was before

Momma died. With her two boys and one more child on the way, Addison stayed busy. Too busy for her little sister. Plus, her husband—who I secretly called Skinny Frank—didn't like me being around much. I couldn't think why.

Unless he knew I was crazy too. Crazy like Momma.

Harper and I chatted until the biscuits were ready, and as soon as she slid one on my plate, I opened the jar of peaches and piled some on the piping-hot biscuit. My fork broke into the crust, and I took a bite and then another until the biscuit and fruit were gone. I was still hungry for more when Harper offered me another, and I didn't say no.

"Thank you for this, Harper. Are you going to stay with us a while? Do you have to go back right away? I thought you would be finished with college by now." I could see a strange expression flutter across her face before she quickly smothered her surprise.

"Aunt Dot didn't tell you?"

"Tell me what, Harper?"

"I would have thought she would have told you."

Harper's question surprised me. I experienced a strange mix of concern and fear. Fear that some other terrible thing was hovering near me. Naturally, I was concerned for my sister, but I was also afraid. Was she going mad too? Did that mean I was doomed to follow in Momma's footsteps? Was Harper suffering from a similar malady?

"Harper? Tell me."

Her face paled, and she put her fork down. "It wasn't anything important, just my leg. I broke it, and it wouldn't heal properly. But I'm much better now."

Harper was lying to me, right to my face.

"You lie, Harper Belle. There are too many secrets in this family! Like what happened to Momma. Do you know what happened to her? Why couldn't we see her? And Aunt Dot wouldn't take me to visit and I wanted to go! Momma came here crying, Harper. After she died. Just ask Aunt Dot! She was crying for me!"

"Loxley…" Harper began when the doorbell rang. She put up her hands as if to instruct me to calm down. That was the story of my life.

Be quiet, Loxley. Don't make a fuss. Calm down!

Harper went to answer the door, but I had had enough of her too. The only way I was going to get some answers was to talk to Momma. Surely, she would be at Summerleigh. I thought Aunt Dot had left the convertible keys since she wasn't driving it today, but they weren't on the ring where she usually hung them. She must have them in her purse. But I had to go. I had to get out of here and go find Momma. I would walk if I had to. *Stupid idea, Loxley. It would take you all day and half the night to walk from here to Summerleigh.* I put my hand on the back door, but I didn't have a chance to leave undetected.

"Loxley, where are you going?" Harper put the plastic Tupperware bowl on the counter. "Please, don't leave." And then her hand quivered and she began to tremble all over. This wasn't merely a case of nerves or something like that. "Lox…ley," she whispered in a rough, broken voice. Harper staggered forward as if to take a seat in the chair, but she didn't make it.

I screamed in horror as her blue eyes began rolling back in her head.

Chapter Five—Jerica

I kept my vision of Loxley to myself. There was too much doubt and unbelief coming from my husband to encourage me to tell him anything much. I could not understand that at all because Jesse knew as well as I did that ghosts did indeed exist and that they had once called Summerleigh home. All the Belles had secrets, in one form or another, but Loxley—I never imagined that she would need my help. From what I knew about the youngest Belle sister, she had been happily married to a young man from Mobile and, besides seeing a few ghosts during her formative years, nothing much troubled her. She seemed so peaceful and happy.

But obviously, I had been wrong.

I managed to fall asleep after seeing her fleeting vision in the mirror of my bathroom. I'd been in absolute shock but managed to keep my composure. Jesse had stayed up reading a crime novel while I tossed and turned. Finally, in the early hours of the morning, I settled down to sleep deeply enough to dream. And in that dream, I wandered about Summerleigh, only I wasn't alone. There were others with me. And then I was somewhere else. But where and with whom? My first thought was, "Marisol!" but it wasn't my daughter at all. I was standing next to Harper and Loxley, although seeing the younger Belle as a teenager was quite a shock. I'd been in the kitchen, but not our kitchen, a smaller one with a shiny red toaster and vintage cherry wallpaper. The girls were arguing, and Harper very clearly had a seizure. In life, I'd never known Harper to have seizures, and I had been her nurse for years. Although that had been a disturbing scene to witness, I knew my old friend had survived and lived many years afterward, but Loxley... The dream only lasted a few seconds and I could hear nothing, only watch the scene unfold. My heart broke for the girls, and I had to get to the bottom of Loxley's sudden appearance in my bathroom and now in my dream. Clearly, Harper wanted me to help her sister. Why else would she come to me like this?

Luckily for me, Jesse's answer to strange things like my seeing our son's carrier slide across the floor or feeling cold spots throughout the house was to offer to take Jordan out for a bit of father-son time. Our son was far too little to comprehend the concept, but I was grateful that Jesse wanted to give me a break. "The gang at the diner would love to see Jordan." He chuckled good-naturedly like we didn't have a care in the world. Like our peaceful home didn't have a half-dozen guests coming in two days. I got the feeling that he wanted to prove to himself that he could actually do the dad thing without Coach Jerica making suggestions. Truth be told, I *had* been a bit of a Helicopter Mom lately, but that was no reason to completely dismiss my experiences.

"Hey, Jess. Don't let Renee give him tea or soda."

"What about beer?" he said with a grin as he shook his head in disbelief. I guess he thought I was joking.

I decided not to argue with him even though I'd personally seen Aunt Ree-Ree attempt to tap a sweet-tea-filled straw near Jordan's mouth. "You two stay out of trouble. What time do you think you'll be back?"

"In a few hours. You know how us Clarke boys run. We're wild ones. Right, Jordan?" he asked as our son yawned his answer. Both of us laughed at that.

"Wow, you've got a live wire on your hands there, sir. Don't make me break out bail money for you two." I kissed Jesse's cheek as I slid the diaper bag up on his shoulder. "Look out, ladies."

Jesse lugged the carrier out to his truck, and I watched them from the doorway. Normally I'd walk the pair out and then supervise the strap job on the car seat and then remind Jesse to drive ten miles under the speed limit, but I didn't do that today. I decided I'd give him the benefit of the doubt even though he hadn't done me the same favor.

Strangely, I felt relieved when they drove away to enjoy their outing. Jordan would be out of harm's way, and I could do what I needed to do to put my mind to rest. And maybe help Loxley.

I bit the inside of my lip as I thought about it. It had been Loxley's name carved in the desk that sparked the first thought of her. The shack, as we now referred to Jesse's newfound writing space, seemed like the natural place to start. Yes, that's what I would do, go back to the shack and check it out without Jesse standing over my shoulder. I didn't want to come off as a snoop—I couldn't care less about his dusty old books and folders stuffed full of notes—but I could feel my senses tingling. And although I wasn't as adept as Hannah with this whole supernatural thing or as in tune as Renee, I trusted my gut. Jesse informed me this morning that Hannah had gone on some kind of retreat. There was no way to get a message to her, and I wouldn't try. Interrupting someone's spiritual retreat was just wrong. Yes, my gut was worth trusting and had not let me down thus far. Bad things happened when I ignored my intuition. Besides, I had to help Loxley, and this was the only way I knew to get started.

I slid on my tennis shoes and dug around the mudroom for my gardening gloves. It was a nice long walk, but I had a wheelbarrow and dozens of flowers to plant. That had been my idea; I just knew some pops of purple and red color would make the shack really look inviting. *Might as well plant them this morning while it's not too hot. After I check out the shack.* The flowers were right where I left them in JB's potting shed. I loaded the wheelbarrow, grabbed my tools and headed down the dirt path to the shack.

Now that we knew the little building was on the property, I couldn't miss it. It's like we always knew it had been there, hidden behind the giant magnolia and a dense forest of shrubs. I was still curious about what this little place had been and who used it. Besides Loxley. Whoever carved that threat into the wood knew she'd see it, and that meant something.

By the time I got to the shack, I was sweaty. I wiped my hands on my cutoff jeans and grabbed my water bottle. After taking a few swigs of water and wiping my brow, I climbed the three steps and went inside to check the place out. As I opened the door and stepped inside, my eyes instantly fell on the big wooden desk. The thing was a monstrosity, really, too big to be in this tiny space. But I knew Jesse would make the most of it. Immediately I made my way to the desk and rubbed my fingers over the carving.

YOU'RE MINE, LOXLEY.

Who would take the trouble to carve something like that? It wasn't a heartwarming message. In fact, it gave me chills. That read like a threat, not a sweet endearment. Not like initials and a heart or an "I love you." That would have been better.

"Loxley, I don't know if you can see me, but I'm here. It's me, Jerica. I helped Harper and Jeopardy. I want to help you too if you'll let me. I see the carving, and I know I saw you in the mirror. Is there something you want to tell me? What can I help you with, Loxley? Show me, please," I pleaded with the image of the teenager that I summoned in my mind.

I didn't take so much as a footstep for fear of setting off a creaking board. If Loxley did make contact with me, I didn't want to miss it. Shoot. Nothing. I paced the room and took a look at Jesse's handiwork; he'd done a marvelous job of replacing boards and sanding damaged pieces. His work had really improved the place already. I tried again and again to make contact with Loxley or Harper, but apparently, nobody wanted to talk to me. Or I wasn't as sharp, in a supernatural sense, as I believed myself to be. With a sigh of frustration, I left the shack and closed the door behind me.

Might as well plant those flowers. I reached for the hoe and began hacking at the hard ground in front of the porch. Jesse and I had removed the overgrown bushes that were clogging up the view, but the ground had been unworked for a while. Probably since John Jeffrey Belle passed away. From the look of the place when we first stumbled on it, Old Ben never so much as stepped inside.

Ah, finally. There was good ground out here after all. My back began to ache, but I ignored the pain and knelt on the ground with the first plant in my hand. With my small shovel,

I created a four-inch hole and eased the flowering bush out of the container and set it in the opening. With some excitement, I arranged the freshly turned soil over the roots and patted around it. *Shoot, I'd forgotten all about water.* Well, luckily the soil had some moisture in it from the rain we had earlier in the week, but I'd have to do something about getting these watered down. I went on to the next plant and then the next. Each time, I used the small shovel to make space for the new plants. Jesse would be tickled to see this newly planted flower garden. I smiled to myself as I did my best to put Loxley out of my mind, at least for a little while.

I reached for another plant and stuck the shovel in the soil again, but I hit something solid. A piece of metal? I put the shovel aside and began to dig with my gloved fingers. Yes, it was a metal container! Digging faster now, I plucked the container out of the ground and brushed off the soil. It was a vintage recipe box, a metal one with litho artwork. I knew this box. Even though the edges had damage and some of the paint was missing, I could clearly see the lobster on the front and the festive salad bowl image on the top. This box had been in the Belle family's kitchen!

I removed my gloves and examined the outside of the box. Yes, this was Ann Marie Belle's—or more to the truth, Harper Belle's—recipe box. Harper had done all the cooking for the family when the girls where young.

When I opened the box, I expected to find a bunch of faded recipe cards and maybe some newspaper cutouts of all the recipes the girls wanted to try, but that's not what I saw. There were no recipes in here, just a collection of trinkets. Some buttons, like the kind you put on a jacket or a backpack.

There was a broken hair clip, an old-fashioned barrette with a bird on it and a sparkling gold bracelet with three charms on it. Each charm was a different musical note symbol. It was a stunning find. I felt a cold chill pass over me as if clouds were gathering above me or someone was walking up on me. I shielded my eyes with my hand and glanced over my shoulder, but I didn't see a soul. And there were no clouds in the sky. I set the box aside and quickly finished my planting job. All the joy from my surprise had vanished. I was focused on the box now and how it got here. Who would hide this recipe box in the yard? During the renovation, we found a few hidey holes in the house, but I didn't think to look in the yard. Could the answer to Loxley's problem be inside this box?

Suddenly, fat raindrops began to fall on me. Where had that cloud come from? Luckily, the planting was done. The shack was beautifully decorated with purple and red flowers, and I felt good about my work here. I put all my tools in the wheelbarrow along with the metal recipe box and began the long walk home. By the time I reached the back porch with the box, I was drenched. I didn't care. Taking off my shoes and hat, I went into the kitchen to get a better look at my surprising find. I wanted to examine all the items in the box; there were quite a few things to look at besides what I'd already seen. I washed my hands and put a towel on the breakfast nook chair. No sense in getting the whole place wet.

Before I could open the box, I heard a woman scream. A long, agonizing scream that shook me to my bones. I jumped out of the chair like a cat on a hot tin roof.

The scream came from upstairs.

Chapter Six—Loxley

Harper and Addison were both home from the hospital, Addison with a new baby. She wouldn't let anyone hold her, which suited me fine since I wasn't skilled at caring for infants. Addison's older children, Earl and Frank Junior, were standoffish too, as if they'd been listening to stories about their crazy aunt and were afraid to speak with me. Harper didn't appear to be bothered by all the hullabaloo, but then again, her new medication tended to make her stare off into space. I knew she wasn't seeing ghosts because there was only one spirit here, and she was hiding on the back patio. That particular ghost didn't like children, which seemed strange since she was Frank's mother. Didn't she realize these children were her own blood?

My nephews whispered to one another like they had the greatest of secrets to share. Addison paid them no mind. She had a girl now, a long-awaited baby that she named Shirley Ellen. Frank Senior, as everyone was now supposed to call him, didn't care for me—or any of us Belles for that matter. Except Addison. He treated Harper and me with quiet suspicion as he smoked his cigarettes and stared at us. But Addison looked as pretty as a picture with her dark hair pulled back in a pink ribbon. She wore pink lipstick and perfectly applied mascara. Like Momma, she wore makeup every day of her life, no matter how sick or how busy.

"Come closer, Loxley. Look at her fingers...aren't they lovely? Who does she look like to you?"

I supposed she wanted me to say Momma, but that would be a lie and I had enough strikes against me as far as heaven went. "You. She looks like you, Addison." My answer apparently satisfied my sister because she smiled and kissed my cheek, which never happened. Frank glowered at me as Aunt Dot helped with the baby. Harper was a sad, crumpled mess on the couch, so I decided to go outside and explore my sister's backyard. It was a small yard, but it had a privacy fence around it. I thought perhaps I could speak to Frank's mother and help her understand that the noisy boys, and now infant girl, were her grandchildren, but she fled from my presence.

I stepped out on the patio and was immediately unimpressed. Addison's rose bushes were trampled down. They must have had a dog at one point. I found his empty, dusty bowl and an old rope in the yard and lots of holes dug in various places. I nearly tripped stepping in a hole that I didn't see when I heard a voice.

"Loxley Belle. Fancy seeing you here." The boy from school smiled at me through a gap in the fence boards.

"Your name is Harmon." It wasn't really a question, more like a statement of surprise. "I know you from school. What are you doing here?"

"That's right. Harmon Gates. Sorry to hear about your mother. I haven't seen you out here before."

I ignored the mention of Momma. The hurt was still too real, and my heart was a tangle of emotions just thinking about it all. "That's because I don't come here often. This is my sister's house. Do you live here? Over there, I mean?"

He smiled even bigger. "No, I'm just visiting. Like you."

"Oh," was all I could think to say to him. I was glad for the conversation, but I didn't have too many friends. Much less of the male persuasion. Making small talk didn't come easy to me.

"Are you..." I spoke as he spoke too. We both laughed at that. Our attempts at talking over one another broke the tension, and I liked him better for having a sense of humor. "Sorry. My sister has a new baby. That's why we're here."

"Congratulations. I don't have any cigars, though." He dug a cigarette out of his jacket pocket and offered me one.

"No, thank you," I said, my like for him shrinking back a bit.

"That's okay. I don't smoke often." He shoved the pack back in his pocket and smoothed back his dark blond hair. He was neatly dressed in dress pants and a clean button-up shirt. I assumed he must be attending a boring family event. Like me. We stood there awkwardly for a moment or two. Ready to bring the conversation to an end, I waved and decided I should ask Aunt Dot to take me home. "I better get back inside."

"But you just got here. Do you really have to go? I was thinking of going for a walk, just around the block. Stretch my legs a bit. What do you say, kiddo?"

I crinkled my nose at him. "Kiddo? My name is Loxley Grace Belle. I'm not a kid. Or a kiddo."

He put his hands up in surrender. With a soft, disarming chuckle, he replied, "I give, Loxley Grace Belle. That has a nice ring to it. My name is Harmon Allen Gates." He extended his hand through the slats in the fence. I shook it briefly and then dropped it like it was a hot potato. "How about that walk?"

"Is that how you ask someone to take a walk with you? I think you have poor manners, Harmon Allen Gates. Offering a lady a cigarette and then calling her 'kiddo.'"

His face took on a serious, hurt expression. "You're probably right, Miss Belle. I'm going to be leaving in a few minutes, anyway. I guess I'll see you at school." As he turned to walk away, I raised my hand and called him back.

"No, wait. Let me check with my Aunt Dot. I don't think she needs me, but I don't want her to wonder where I am."

He smiled, and it was a beautiful sight. Funny, I didn't think of Harmon as handsome at all when I first met him, but he was kind of cute. Not dreamy like Frank Sinatra but certainly nice to look at. "I will be out front unless you prefer that I meet you down the street."

"No need for that. My aunt isn't overprotective. She loves it when I participate in social activities, and I certainly think this would qualify. I'll be there in a minute."

Sure enough, Aunt Dot had no objections to my meeting a school friend out on the street. In fact, she seemed pleased as punch about the whole thing and didn't bother to ask me if the friend was a girl or a boy. I didn't feel inclined to tell her. I shrugged as she held the crying baby and walked around the room with her. Earlier, Frank had been trying to take photographs with his big, black camera, Frank was a newspaperman, or so he fancied himself. But he wasn't satisfied with any of the shots. I'd not been asked to be in any of them. The poor baby wasn't pleased at all with anything they were trying to do. Shirley Ellen screamed at the top of her lungs, but at least the sound had Harper's attention.

"Would you like to walk with me and my friend, Harper?"

"No, I'm going to hold the baby. Just look at her—isn't she beautiful? Give her to me, Aunt Dot. It's my turn." I didn't agree or disagree but went about my merry way.

"Be back in an hour, Loxley. We have to go home and get started on those thank-you cards," my aunt reminded me as she carefully deposited the baby in Harper's arms. Addison sat beside her; I wondered how long that would last. I stepped outside and hurried down the sidewalk to meet Harmon. My brother-in-law followed me out and watched me walk away with my schoolmate. I pretended that his staring didn't bother me. I guess it really shouldn't have, but for some reason it did. His disapproval was clear, but I didn't owe him any explanation.

"Who is that scarecrow?" Harmon asked. "Don't tell me that's your dad."

I huffed at him and hot-footed it away from my brother-in-law's house as fast as possible. I didn't glance back once.

Chapter Seven—Loxley

"No, my dad died a long time ago. That scarecrow is my brother-in-law, Frank. You don't know him? He is your neighbor," I said as I shoved my hands in my skirt pockets. They were noticeably empty; I'd been a good girl lately, but how long would that last? The feeling of powerlessness grew by the day, and I knew it was only a matter of time before I found and took another treasure.

"Sorry about that. I didn't mean to offend you. He's not my neighbor, though. I have never seen him before."

We walked under a moss-covered oak along broken sidewalks. Our footsteps matched almost perfectly, and for some reason that made me even more comfortable with Harmon Gates. This really was a nice neighborhood with rows of modest yet modern houses. And it was such a beautiful day that people were outside enjoying the pleasant afternoon. A few of them greeted us, while others just stared. I wasn't sure how far Harmon planned to walk, but I wasn't in a hurry. An hour could be a long time or a short time, depending on whose company you spent it in. Funny, I didn't think it weird at all that I would spend time with a boy who was practically a stranger.

"If that's not your house, what were you doing there, pray tell?"

"Pray tell? Did you pick that up from Mrs. Givens? I never heard that until I moved to George County."

I noticed that he didn't directly answer me, but I wasn't going to pry. I took the opening to talk about a class we were in together, and we joked about how Mrs. Givens stuttered occasionally, especially when she got upset about any old thing. For example, if she caught someone chewing gum, she'd just about blow a gasket. That was a phrase I picked up from one of Harper's old boyfriends. We chatted for a while, and the hour passed far more quickly than I imagined it would.

"Golly, I've got to get back. Aren't your parents expecting you? I don't normally have a curfew, but like I said, I don't live here. We live over off Highway 63."

"I thought you lived off Hurlette," he said as we began to walk back to Addison's place. Again, he didn't answer my question, and that was beginning to bother me. I didn't enjoy secrets too much, even though I had quite a few of my own. How did he know about Summerleigh? Had he been listening to gossip? I stopped on the sidewalk, feeling like the world was crashing down around me. I shoved my hands back in my pockets.

"What do you know about Hurlette? Or me?"

"I've seen the house—I've seen Summerleigh. I got lost when I first moved out here. I drove down the road and saw the house. It's the only house on Hurlette, except that small one at the end of the drive. The Richardson place, I think." I felt a little sick as he continued, "It's common knowledge that your family owns that big old place. I thought I saw you there."

"You were spying on me, Harmon Gates?" I didn't offer up any information. All the pleasantness of the conversation had vanished, and the evening shadows were gathering. I could hear Aunt Dot calling me in the distance, and I began walking faster and away from Harmon.

"Of course not. Wait a second. Did I offend you? Please, wait." His tone was softer than I'd heard all afternoon, so I did as he asked. I turned around and pretended that there weren't tears in my eyes. "I did offend you, but why?"

"I'm not answering any more of your questions, Harmon. You haven't answered any of mine. There are plenty of busybodies around this town and at our school. I'm sure you've been listening to them. Well, believe what you want—I don't care!"

Harmon lightly touched my arm and stepped closer, and I didn't back away. I did pull my arm away, though. I didn't like being touched much. When I was little, I loved being held and toted around. Not anymore.

"I don't spend much time with busybodies. In case you haven't noticed, I'm not the most popular kid in school. I'd like to be your friend—I really would. Listen, I know how they treat you, that prissy girl and her smarmy friends, and I don't like it. I don't think it is right. If she were a guy, I'd punch her in the nose. But I'm a stranger here, and I don't have too many buddies either. If you think the girls are bad, you should try being friends with these hard-ass rednecks."

I was surprised at Harmon's use of profanity, but I felt it too. I wasn't sure how I felt about Harmon or anyone right now. I was still reeling from Momma's loss. Talking about school wasn't making me feel any better.

"Hardly any of those guys own a car, but I'm gonna soon. Do you like cars?"

"Yes. Where are you from, Harmon? Not Mississippi, for sure."

"Georgia," he said without a hint of a smile on his face.

"Do you lie about everything? You ain't from Georgia either."

His eyes were fixed on mine like he was trying to decide if he could trust me. I darn sure didn't trust Harmon Gates, but that didn't mean he couldn't be my friend.

"You got me. I'm from California. San Diego, actually. Have you heard of it?"

I gasped at his perception of me. "Of course I have. I'm not a redneck yahoo or whatever you called it. I can read a map, and I have a car too. Well, share one. I drive my aunt's car sometimes. It's a convertible."

"Nice."

Harmon's smile was affecting me in strange yet not unpleasant ways. I swallowed and said, "I better go. I can hear Aunt Dot calling me. She must be ready to go home. Want to walk with me? Don't you live nearby?"

He smiled and shook his head. "No, I don't live this way. I was just doing a mechanical job for someone. I better go, toots." I couldn't figure out why, but I knew he was lying to me. And poorly. Who worked on cars in dress clothes? There wasn't any grease under his fingernails, either. Daddy always had grease under his nails. Harmon caught me looking and smiled. "I took a shower. I clean up pretty good, huh?"

"I suppose so, but I'm not a toots either. It's Loxley or nothing."

"Loxley it is. No more nicknames. I'll see you at school, then." Harmon dug a cigarette out of his pocket, put it in his mouth and lit it as he walked away.

What a strange boy. I wasn't sure I wanted a friend who smoked cigarettes, but beggars can't be choosers. Aunt Dot impatiently waited for me on the porch, but as soon as she saw me, her anxious expression vanished. She really was the nicest person on the planet. "There you are. I was about to call the police department. Harper is already in the car. That medicine makes her sleepy, and the baby is worn slap out. Do you want to go inside and say goodbye to your sister? I hate to run off, but Harper has another doctor's appointment in the morning."

"No, ma'am. I'm ready to go home. What's for supper?"

"Cold chicken. Are you going to help me with the thank-you cards?"

"Yes, I'll be glad to help you."

We climbed in the car, and I was surprised to see Harper sitting in the back seat. Her lovely eyes were blank and staring at nothing. I hoped she got better soon. I missed my vivacious, fun-loving sister. Aunt Dot said she would improve, that the seizures wouldn't come back, but at what cost? Harper had moments of lucidity, but they were few and far between. As she backed out of the driveway, Aunt Dot said, "Frank said you were walking with a boy. Is that true?" Her sunshiny voice relayed her excitement at the idea that I might have a boyfriend.

"He is just a friend from school. I wasn't lying about it."

"Oh, I never thought you were lying. What's his name, dear?"

"Harmon Gates, but you wouldn't know him. He's new to the county. Aunt Dot! Look out!" A small white poodle with a child following him raced out in front of us. My aunt slammed on the brakes, and I whacked my head on the dashboard.

"Loxley? Let me take a look, sweetheart." Aunt Dot dug a handkerchief out of her purse while the child and his dog scampered away. "Oh, shoot. You might need a stitch or two. Harper, are you okay?"

Harper didn't make a sound, but there were tears in her eyes, unshed and just hanging out there making her eyes glassy. Kind of like my teddy bear's eyes. I accepted the handkerchief as some rude person behind us blew their horn. I glanced in the side mirror, surprised to see Harmon's face smiling back at me.

"That's Harmon! That's my friend from school," I confessed as I swiveled around in the seat with the cloth pressed to my head. I don't know why, but I waved like an idiot. He waved back and flicked his cigarette out the window as he eased past us.

Aunt Dot frowned at him and then at me, but she didn't scold me as she shifted into gear and took us home. We practically crawled down the highway; she was gun-shy about the near accident now. I assured her that I was fine and didn't need stitches.

"If you change your mind, we can go right up to Dr. Lamb's office. I'm sure he'd stitch you up in no time."

"No, thank you. I don't want to go to the dance with stitches in my forehead." Just as the words came out of my mouth, I knew that I *would* go to the dance. For the first time ever, I would attend a dance, and I would go with Harmon Gates. He was going to ask me—I was sure of that. And if he didn't, I would ask him. Aunt Dot's enthusiasm concerning the dance had clearly waned since she got a peek at my intended date. She didn't openly object, but she began making excuses for me.

"If you don't want to go, I understand, dear. It's been a very difficult time, and the grieving process takes a while. It's different for everyone."

"I'm sure it is, Aunt Dot, but I'm going to the dance. All the seniors go."

We drove the rest of the way very slowly and in complete silence.

Chapter Eight—Jerica

"Jordan, please go to sleep," I pleaded with my child as I rubbed his back and paced the downstairs hallway. A major storm raged above us, complete with house-rattling thunderclaps and the occasional pop of lightning. I thought lightning had struck one of the peach trees in the backyard, but I wasn't brave enough to stand by the window yet to check. As soon as the lights went out, I was up. My tiny nightstand fan quit blowing, and I could hear every creak of the house. And then Jordan woke up too. At least I'd gotten in a few hours of sleep before all hell broke loose over the house.

"It's okay, baby. It's just a storm. It will pass soon. I promise," I whispered hopefully as I took another lap up and down the hall. The room filled with blue light as the thunder rolled again. The LED candles I'd switched on were enough to make the downstairs parlor less frightening, but the rest of the house was completely black. I prayed the power would come back on soon. My cell phone had been charging in the bedroom, but I couldn't manage to bring it with me while I held a wiggling child in my arms. Oh well, who was I going to call? Jesse would be sound asleep right now. He was away overnight at a book signing, but he'd be asleep even if he were here, unless I purposefully woke him up. It was surprising how heavily men could sleep. Eddie was much the same way when Marisol was a baby.

Oh, Marisol, baby girl. I miss you so much.

I held Jordan a little tighter and kissed his cheek. He'd worked himself up into a sweat and would be ready to crash soon. Hopefully. Maybe I'd get a few hours in too. At least there was no screaming woman roaming the halls tonight. I couldn't believe I'd heard such a horrible, bloodcurdling sound in my own home, but I had found nothing to account for it. I'd looked everywhere to find the source, but there was no one about, not in the house or outside, and the closest neighbor was a half a mile away. Whatever had caused it, I would never forget it. I decided to try the recliner again. Jordan much preferred walking, but I was exhausted. After a few minutes of singing and humming, he began to settle down. He yawned a few times and then got quiet despite the warm temperature. I wanted to drift off too and enjoy at least a nap, but I had an odd, uncomfortable feeling. Like someone was watching me. Grinning at me.

You're just being weird, Jerica.

The feeling didn't go away. Not at all. In fact, the longer I sat in the darkness, the more intensely I experienced it. I could see right through the parlor and had a straight shot to the back door, but it was so dark out that I couldn't make out a thing.

Don't be a child. Go take a look.

My arms tingled a bit; I'd been holding my son for an hour. Time to give my arms and eyes a break, but first I had to know if someone was out there. I had to be sure.

There! I saw a shadow move past the back window. I know I saw it. I froze and waited to see if the figure would return. If I saw the shadow again, I'd have to call someone. Jordan didn't stir at all as I tiptoed toward the back door ever so slowly. Even though it was nearly pitch black in this section of the house, I managed not to kick the coffee table or any other furniture. I stood in the doorway of the kitchen and waited.

Nothing. I didn't see anything at all now except for darkness. After a minute of hovering in the doorway, I stepped into the kitchen. There was no one in here except Jordan and me. Everything was as I left it. The kitchen was tidy with a few clean dishes in the drain. I had some flameless candles in here too, but I couldn't manage flicking those on with my baby in my arms. I blinked against the darkness, and my eyes began adjusting to the lack of light. No, everything was as it should be.

Except for the recipe box. The one I'd found in the flowerbed yesterday.

I'd had every intention of reopening the recipe box, but that scream... That horrible scream had shaken me so badly that I'd been forced to put it away. For reasons unknown to me, I actually hid the thing instead of sharing it with Jesse. *That's right. I'd hidden it! Why was it here?* Nobody had been in here except the baby and me. Jesse had left this morning and didn't know anything about it. I hadn't mentioned it to him, and then he got the sudden phone call inviting him to participate in the book signing. Those were rare for him nowadays, so I had encouraged him to go.

And now the recipe box was open. It was open and on the table. Jordan whimpered in his sleep but didn't wake up fully. I stepped back and away from the table. I didn't want to be in here. Not anymore. I had to call someone. Who? I had to tell someone about this. I should have already told Jesse about the recipe box. *Okay, think reasonably, Jerica.*

Maybe Renee had come over earlier. She'd promised she was going to help me get ready for this weekend. That was probably it. Renee must have found the recipe box, gotten curious about it and opened it up.

That's a lie, Jerica Clarke, and you know it. Renee would never just come inside without saying anything to you. She wouldn't do that. Never ever.

Lightning snapped again but without the thunder. "That's odd," I said, feeling confused about everything that was happening. And then a flurry of shadows rushed past the door. Clutching the baby in my arms, I hurried out of the kitchen and with a pounding heart began climbing the stairs. As soon as I reached the second-floor landing, I glanced behind me in the dark. I didn't see anything at all, but that horrible feeling of being watched was slow to leave me. By the time I made it halfway down the hall, I felt better...like I'd left whatever it was downstairs. It wasn't inside the house, at least. It must have just been shadows! I carefully navigated the dim hallway and went into Jordan's room. *Breathe, Jerica. Just breathe.* I didn't hear anything, no sound of breaking glass. Nothing to indicate that anything I saw was more than just the odd grouping of shadows. What to compare that experience to? The shadow wasn't just an anomalous blob of darkness. Not the waving of a tree branch or even the shadow of a single person. It was like several people were lumped together, but there were no defining features. No arms and legs. More like three lumps, three people with sheets over their heads. Black sheets. I put the baby down and toyed with the idea of opening a window, but I couldn't do it. I just couldn't. What if the shadow things could crawl up the side of the house and come through a window? Clearly, it couldn't come inside. Or else it would have, right? What time was it, anyway? God, it was hot. But I had to go back downstairs and check it out, just in case. I felt my way back to the door when suddenly the lights flickered back on.

Breathing a sigh of relief, I took a peek at Jordan and went back to the staircase. No. I had no weird feeling here. Maybe I'd been hallucinating. The recipe box was tucked in the cabinet. There had been no shadow peeking in my back door. Lack of sleep could make you see weird things, right? And it had been so dark. So very dark.

I headed back down the stairs to verify what I'd seen. There was the memory of that feeling, but I didn't sense anyone grinning at me now. Passing through the parlor, I returned to the kitchen to find that the recipe box was open. All of the contents had been poured out on the counter. The barrette, the paper clip and all the other odd things were right here. No, wait a second... I picked up the dirty tin to verify that it was empty. Not everything was here; one thing was missing. The most valuable item in the recipe box.

The charm bracelet had vanished.

Chapter Nine—Loxley

"You know, they say lots of intelligent people had seizures. Julius Caesar, for one," I said awkwardly as Harper tied my ribbon. If she'd asked, I wouldn't have been able to drum up another name. Harper never made eye contact with me, but I wanted to talk about so many things. Aunt Dot was in her room putting the finishing touches on her hair and makeup; I was quite glad she would be a chaperone tonight even though some people thought it a tad scandalous for me to go to a dance so soon after Momma's funeral. Then again, people were always talking about us. Or at least me. I would think it strange if they didn't at this point.

"Harper, did you hear me? Having a seizure isn't the end of the world. This isn't the nineteenth century, you know," I commented as I tried to catch her attention in the mirror. She moved slowly, and her face and lips were pale. I'm sure I was being rude, but I didn't know how else to bring up the subject. I needed to talk about something besides my own crimes and Momma's death. My sister wasn't herself anymore; at first, I blamed it on the medication, but now I wasn't so sure it was merely that. Harper was unusually quiet tonight. She was leaving on Sunday, which gave us only a couple more days to spend time together. At least she had stayed longer than she first planned. Maybe this dance was a selfish idea, but I couldn't let Harmon down now that I'd promised to go with him. I'd been right, of course. He'd asked me to go just two days after I'd taken that first walk with him.

To my surprise, my sister tiptoed to the door and closed it. Then she turned the radio on low. Some goofy commercial played as I spun around just in time for her to catch my hands and pull me down from the stool. We sat together on the round cushioned seat. It had seemed a strange idea to have this particular piece of furniture in my room when Aunt Dot first suggested it, but now it just seemed right. It belonged here.

"I have to find Jeopardy. I promised I would find her. Is she at Summerleigh? Have you seen her? I don't want you to go without me. We have to stick together. Don't go without me, okay?" Harper said through dry lips. Her eyes still had that glassy look about them, but she was serious. Dead serious. Clearly, Jeopardy weighed on her mind. Harper had barely spoken two words to me since her seizure after Momma's funeral, and now she wanted to go home? This wasn't what I expected from her. I thought perhaps she was going to warn me about Harmon, about not kissing him or letting him get to first base, and I wouldn't have minded if she had warned me. Someone needed to. My life was threatening to spin out of control, and I was already feeling the need to regain some power over it in the only way I knew how. What would I find next to add to my treasure collection?

"You can go with me, Harper. We have every right to be there—it is our home. Summerleigh will always be home to us. I know bad things happened from time to time, I remember some of it, but we had some happy times too. Remember the kittens and Jeopardy's castle room? Don't you remember?"

"Have you seen Jep? Please tell me the truth." Harper's eyes narrowed and her lips quivered at the mention of our lost sister's name.

"I have never seen her, Harper. Never. I saw a girl once, but she was transparent. She didn't have any color to her at all and disappeared in the hallway. I don't think it was Jeopardy."

Harper collapsed on the round couch and rocked back and forth with tears in her eyes. To this day, she couldn't let Jeopardy go. She was obsessed with finding our sister and bringing her home. I wanted Jeopardy home too, but that wouldn't fix things. Our family was broken, too broken for anything to be right ever again.

Desperation kindled spontaneous tears of sympathy. "Harper, please. Don't leave me. Don't go back to Birmingham. I think I'll die if you leave me again. You don't know what I've done, Harper. You just don't know." My sister smoothed my hair with her hand. "Jeopardy is gone, probably ran off with that boy from the carnival, you know it's true. And then Addison married Skinny Frank, and I don't have anyone. I'll die if you leave me, Harper."

Panicked now, Harper hugged me tightly and whispered, "You won't die. I'm not leaving forever. Just a little while. You're doing so well, Loxley. I used to feel guilty that I left you with Aunt Dot, but now I see that it really is for the best. She loves you. She loves you better than any of us, I think."

"Why are you crying? What's happened?" Aunt Dot barreled into my room without knocking, and that's when I realized she'd been crying too. She crouched down beside us and held us both, and although I'm sure she would have loved an answer to her question, we didn't have one to give her. "Just look at you, Loxley. You look like a model out of a magazine. You're just lovely. Isn't she beautiful, Harper?"

Before my sister could answer, a car honked in the driveway. I couldn't imagine who it was. Aunt Dot didn't date, and Harper didn't seem interested in anyone, much to the dismay of one Ben Hartley, who hung the moon and stars on her every look in his direction. Imagine attending a funeral just to stare at her? I wiped my eyes as I watched the big blue car pull into the driveway. I guess Harmon had gotten that car after all.

But how in the world did he know where Aunt Dot and I lived? I never asked him to pick me up, not once. I just assumed he and I would meet up at the dance. Yes, I couldn't help but smile at seeing tall, lean Harmon step out of the car and button his black jacket. I hardly recognized him with his slicked-back hair and proper suit. Mind you, he never looked a slouch, but he never really dressed up either. We'd gotten to know one another pretty well in the two weeks since Momma's funeral. We ate all our lunches together, he helped me with a paper for Givens' class, and I helped him with math. He was as secretive as he always was...I felt so comfortable with him that it didn't really matter. But I was curious, for sure. Maybe a little more than curious, to be honest. He never talked about his parents; he did mention his brother-in-law and sister a few times, but I got the feeling he wasn't too connected with either of them.

"Good evening, Miss Daughdrill. Miss Belle. My name is Harmon. I'm very pleased to meet you. You look a sight, Loxley Belle. I am a lucky fellow. May I drive you to the dance? With your permission, of course, Miss Daughdrill?" Harmon's polite tone caught my aunt off-kilter. I could see that she was prepared to go full tilt on him for presuming to honk in the driveway. Thankfully, my sweet aunt wasn't one to embarrass me, but she had her hand on her hip—a sure sign that she didn't like this at all.

"I don't know, Harmon. I am a chaperone for the school dance. I had planned on taking my niece and bringing her home."

"I certainly don't mean to make trouble, ma'am." Harmon bowed his head slightly and turned to leave. "I came by early to ask if Loxley might go for a soda with me before the dance. A few of the other kids are going."

"Aunt Dot," I whispered like a freight train. "Please," I added with a pitiful expression and a voice that reminded her that this had been what she wanted. My aunt was always on me to turn off the radio and go be with people my own age, make new friends.

"Alright, young man, but you must have my niece home by eleven o'clock. No later than that, and I do not like young men honking their car horns in the driveway. Next time, please walk to the door. That is what a gentleman would do." Aunt Dot flushed beneath her thick layer of makeup. She wore it just for the occasion, and I suddenly felt a little guilty about not riding with her to the dance.

"Yes, ma'am. I do apologize for my behavior. I suppose I was just a little excited. Please accept my apologies. Loxley? May I?" Harmon extended his hand, and I couldn't help but melt at the gesture. Nobody had ever taken me to a dance before or offered me their hand or anything else romantic like that. I suddenly felt very afraid about riding with Harmon, who wasn't much more than a stranger.

"I will see you at the dance." My aunt smiled, but it wasn't a trusting smile. It was the same kind of smile she used whenever she thought the man behind the meat counter shorted her on her roast beef order. My sister stared at me like a life-size doll and slid her arm through our aunt's arm. Was she crying again?

"Bye, Loxley. I'll wait up for you," Harper said sweetly in her dreamy voice.

"Bye, Harper! Bye, Aunt Dot!"

Harmon swung the car door open elegantly and waited for me to ease my fluffy skirt inside and spread it out before he closed the door. I could hardly believe this was happening. I had never imagined that I would be escorted to the dance in such beautiful style. With waves and smiles, we left the driveway and headed toward our high school.

Chapter Ten—Jerica

"I knew you were holding out on me, Jerica Clarke. What's been going on? The energy here at Summerleigh has shifted, seriously shifted. It's almost frenetic. Have you seen Harper? Why would she come back?" Renee arranged the guest towels on the freshly made bed as I moved the jar of fresh-cut flowers from the nightstand to the dresser. Some people had flower allergies, and I didn't want to risk a guest having an allergy attack. They were supposed to tell us about those sorts of things when they made their reservations, but people didn't always think about it. The nagging ache in my back returned as I bent over to arrange the throw pillows. I had my son in his baby backpack carrier, only he was on the front of my body, not my back. I wanted to keep my eyes on him. I hadn't put him back in that car carrier since the incident in the kitchen.

"This is the last room. Now to make sure I have everything I need in the fridge for breakfast and lunch for two days."

"Nice try. You can't avoid the question. What's going on?"

As we left the room—this would have been Loxley and Addison's room—I closed the door and dropped my voice. "The baby's carrier slid across the floor in the kitchen. He's scared, and I worry every second that he's being...toyed with."

"What? None of the Belles would hurt him. The only one who would have done anything like that was Ann Marie, and

"

she's gone. We all witnessed her leaving. Who is it that you think is here?"

I glanced at Loxley's door and rubbed my sleeping baby's back as we went back to the front room.

"Loxley or Addison?"

I sat on the couch and leaned back against the pillow. I was a sweaty mess, but Summerleigh was mostly ready for visitors. "We found an inscription in Jesse's writer shack. It said, 'You're mine, Loxley.'"

"What? Why didn't you tell me?"

"I don't know. Jesse wants to put all that ghost stuff behind us, but it seems the ghosts aren't done yet. I heard a scream the other day when I was opening that recipe box. I found it in the dirt in front of the shack. It used to belong to the Belle family. I know Harper used it a number of times."

"And? Go on," Renee said as she twisted her dark hair back up into a messy bun. Her makeup was a bit runny under her eyes. She'd worked herself into a sweat too, apparently.

"Inside the recipe box were a bunch of things. A barrette, some coins, a paper clip. But also one thing in particular that was unusual—a gold charm bracelet with musical note charms. When I heard the scream, I went upstairs to see who was there but didn't find anyone. It shook me up so bad that I put everything back in the box and stuck it in the cabinet by the phone."

"I have to see it," she announced as she headed to the cabinet, then she came back with the rusty-edged box and opened it up. She dumped the contents on the coffee table and handled each one. "Interesting. It's a shame that Hannah can't be here, but we can do this. We can figure out what it is she wants. But who is she? You know, if you give me a few minutes, maybe an hour or two, I could try to make contact."

"Not with Jordan here, Aunt Ree-Ree. Besides, something is already trying to make contact, and I don't like the way he or she is going about it. Or whatever it is."

Renee picked up the box and turned it upside down. "Where's the charm bracelet? I don't see it in here. You say it was gold?" She carefully sifted through the items on the table, her dark eyebrow raised slightly as she studied each one.

"It disappeared. Someone opened the box and took it and left the rest of the stuff on the table. Last night when the power went out."

"Jesse, maybe? No early guests?"

I gave her a look that said, "Really?"

"Okay, so wow. That means someone doesn't want you to have it. Maybe we should put the box back in the ground."

"Without the charm bracelet? I don't know what is going on here. Oh, shoot. The phone is ringing. Would you get it for me? My back is killing me."

"Sure," she said as I began putting everything back in the recipe box. Didn't need this lying out here. The guests would be here soon. I really needed to get my hair in order.

"It's Jesse. Take the phone and let me unhook you. I'll put Jordan in his bed and stay with him."

"Thanks," I said with some relief as she unhooked my backpack and carried my sleeping lump of a baby upstairs. *That's right, kid. Sleep all day, scream all night.* I hoped he didn't disturb the guests. Nothing like trying to keep B & B guests happy with a screaming kid in the house.

"Hi, beautiful. How are things?"

"Magical," I said with a chuckle. That was the term we used when things just went completely crazy.

"So magical that you need me to come right this minute? I will if you need me."

"I need you to sell some books, truckloads. The house is ready, thanks to Renee. Your son doesn't like to sleep at night." *That and I saw shadows outside the back door and the power went out for an hour or two last night.*

"I'm leaving at two; I'll be home around four. I thought I might have the opportunity to stay another day, but I've not been invited. It's been a great book expo. I had no idea so many people were waiting for my next book. We've got to finish working on that shack so I can get started."

"Slow down there, Jesse Clarke. One thing at a time. The guests are coming in tonight, so I'll definitely need you here at least by four. I'm happy you're making such great connections with your fans, but I think I told you that you needed to get started writing. That was me, right?"

"Yes, that was you. And you were right. You usually are, but I love you anyway, Jerica Clarke."

"Hey..." I pretended to be irritated by his suggestion that I felt I had to be right all the time. I didn't think that at all.

"Kiss Jordan for me."

"I will. He's upstairs with his aunt right at the moment. Be safe, and we'll see you around four o'clock." He didn't ask me about ghosts or moving baby carriers, and I didn't bring it up.

"Bye, Jerica." He hung up the phone as the doorbell rang. *Oh no, please tell me they aren't early.*

Chapter Eleven—Jerica

I caught a glimpse of myself from the mirror and was appalled. No time to doctor that hair up. I smoothed out my clothes and opened the door to find four smiling, tired faces. Well, no harm. They were only an hour early.

"Hi, everyone. Welcome to Summerleigh." I smiled at them and held the door open so they could come inside and out of the heat.

"You must be Jerica Clarke. I know we're early, but we thought maybe we could leave our luggage here and head out for a little while. Harry's got a lead foot, and we got here faster than we expected. I'm Trisha Beckett. This is my husband, Harry. And this is my sister, Karen, and her husband, Ron."

I immediately liked them. They were tired but seemed to be a fun-loving group. That was good. It sucked having hard-to-please visitors.

"Actually, your rooms are ready now. If you'll follow me." I waved them toward the hallway.

"Wow, this place is beautiful. I could put two of my apartments in here," Trisha commented as I led them through the front room and to Loxley's room. I opened the door and gasped before closing it again. Loxley's bedroom was a disaster. The sheets and blankets had been torn off the bed, and the fresh-cut flowers were on the floor. It looked like someone had thrown a fit during the brief time since Renee and I had left the room.

I pointed to the next door down. "Um, wrong room. This is the one," I lied as best I could. The guests didn't argue with me, but Trisha raised an eyebrow. I opened the door and let the first couple walk in. "The Wisteria Room. The bathroom is just beyond."

"I call dibs," Trisha shouted as she put her luggage on the floor and walked around the room. "Wow, it's a beautiful room."

I managed to smile at her even though I was dying inside. "Karen and Ron, you're in the room at the end of the hall." I opened the door to the Rose Room and quietly breathed a sigh of relief. Everything was in order in Ann Marie Belle's old room. The wrought-iron bed was perfectly made up and looked so inviting. The rose quilt was folded neatly, the soft towels piled up on the end of the bed. Thank goodness not all the rooms were destroyed. I left our guests to get acquainted with their weekend digs and walked upstairs to find Renee.

"Our guests are here."

"Great," Renee said as she wound up the mobile again. My son was wide awake now. He must have gotten his nap in while I carried him around this afternoon.

"Not great. I mean, I don't mind that they came early, but Loxley's room is tore up."

"What?"

"Yeah, tore up. I mean, the bed is unmade and the flowers are strewn all over the ground. It looks like someone had a hissy fit and decided to undo all our work." I paced the floor as I cracked my knuckles.

Renee said, "I have to go see this for myself."

"Okay," was all I could think to say. A few minutes later, Renee was back, her face equally pale and filled with confusion. "You saw it?"

"Yes, but I don't understand it."

"Do you think the guests will be okay? Jesse says he'll be home around four o'clock."

Renee snorted. "And what's he going to do? You know he's about as sensitive as a mud hole. Spiritually speaking. But you should tell him, whether he wants to hear it or not. In the meantime, you've got guests to take care of. Why don't you let me take Jordan home with me? Uncle Frank and I would love to have him for an overnight."

I bit my fingernail thinking about that proposal. "He's a night owl, Renee. And he's not much for staying on schedule. Frank isn't going to appreciate being kept up all night. You won't either when it's two in the morning and Jordan is screaming like a banshee."

"You let me worry about that. If I have any trouble, I'll call you. Scout's honor."

"Alright, but don't hesitate to call me, please." We packed Jordan's overnight bag, which included a ridiculous amount of diapers.

"Really? That many?"

I laughed at her lack of faith in my child's ability to pee on everything. "Yes, really. And use caution when removing his diaper. Call me tonight, okay?"

"Bye, Helicopter Mom."

I winced at the name, but I owned it. I really was too overprotective, but losing one child had nearly killed me. *You're being ridiculous, Jerica. Let him go have fun with Renee. She loves him like he's her own.*

I stuffed the bag with bottles and everything I could think of and watched them leave. My guests had left too, and I was now alone in Summerleigh.

Or at least I thought I was. I was about to find out how wrong I could be.

Chapter Twelve—Loxley

I had never seen so much glitter in my life. Every paper star that hung from the gymnasium ceiling was covered in the blue shiny stuff, and what I once thought was hokey was actually quite lovely. Magical, even. Here I was with a handsome date; yes, Harmon Gates was a nice-looking guy. Tonight, he looked every bit as hunky as Chuck Welford, Shannon Bohannan's date.

"Everyone is watching us, Loxley Belle," Harmon whispered in my ear. I liked the feel of his breath on my skin, but there was also a part of me that was uncomfortable with his intimate proximity. "Do you know why they are whispering?"

"No, I mean, yes. I think I should go home now, Harmon. Please take me home." Music began to play, and it was a song I knew and loved. The bandleader sang a Perry Como song, *No other love have I...* And even though I had never danced with a boy before in my life, I didn't step on his toes as he politely put his hands in mine and smiled down at me.

Watching the night go by. Wishing that you could be watching the night with me...

"They are looking at you because you are the most beautiful girl at George County High School. You're the most beautiful girl in this whole school, and I am one lucky guy."

I couldn't help but smile at Harmon. His dark eyes and olive skin made him look so exotic, like a movie star. Well, he was from California, if one believed him. Was Hollywood anywhere near San Diego?

"Harmon..." I couldn't look into those eyes any longer. It wasn't right for me to have the feelings I was having right now. I barely knew him.

"One day, you'll look back on this night and say that Harmon was right. He was right that night, and I didn't believe him. Believe me, Loxley Belle. I have never said this to another girl, and I am sure I will never say it again, but I have to tell you this because I don't know when I'll have another chance. I leave tomorrow."

"You're playing games with me, Harmon, and I don't like it." I glowered at him, but his intense expression didn't change. The couples on the dance floor began to clap as the song ended. To my surprise, all the chaperones took the dance floor, including Aunt Dot. To my further shock, Aunt Dot was dancing with Mr. Maurice Patrick, our new football coach. Coach Patrick was a handsome man and never gave the schoolgirls so much as a second look, not even the seniors, but he certainly appeared interested in my Aunt Dot. She was caught up in his arms, and they danced to an old Count Basie song.

I want a little girl to love a lot...

"Loxley Grace Belle? Are you listening to me?"

"You don't even know me, Harmon. You really don't. I am crazy, just like they say I am," I said as I peeked over his shoulder at Aunt Dot, who was enraptured in Coach Patrick's whispered words. Oh, yes, Aunt Dot was in love. That was plain now. How could I have missed it? Was that why the girls all hated me so ferociously?

No, it's because you're evil, Loxley Grace. Just plain old evil. Like your crazy Momma.

"I know you are different from the rest of these George County girls. You don't treat people badly. Not on purpose. You take things from time to time, but it's like a tic you have...you know, a habit. I don't care about that because I love you. I know that about you, but I don't care. There, I said it. I love you!"

I was staring at him in shock, for many reasons. He said he loved me. Me, Loxley Grace Belle. And there was something else—he knew my secret, or at least part of my secret, but that meant he knew too much. Oh, so that was it. Harmon must have seen me collect that charm bracelet. He must have seen me pick up Betty Lou's barrette the day before. He knew my secrets—what did he want from me?

You don't know just how different I am. Tears crowded my eyes but did not fall. How could the most beautiful night of my life be marred by my own sins? Sins that others had witnessed. As I fought back the tears, and the two of us stood in the center of that gymnasium staring at one another, the band started playing *Stranger in Paradise.*

"That's you, Loxley. You're my paradise." Girls walked past us, couples hand in hand. Harmon and I didn't hold hands, even though he offered his to me now. I had no idea where Aunt Dot was, either. "It's okay if you don't love me. I love you. I do, Loxley. What would you say if I told you I was leaving this one-horse town? You could go with me. We could be together, always."

"What do you mean? You just got here," I said as I took his hands in my own. "Are you joking with me, Harmon?"

"No, I wish I were. My brother-in-law is leaving soon, him and my sister. I live with them, Loxley. So... I have to go when they go."

I dropped his hands, and tears began to fall. This all seemed so improbable. "No, you don't. You have a car, and you could stay and get a job. You could be your own man. We're about to graduate, for Pete's sake. What about me? You say you love me, but you tell me you're going to leave?" My voice was rising, but I didn't care who heard us.

"Who is going to hire me? If I don't have Nancy and Simon's help, I don't have anything. And where I come from, family sticks together. Always."

I took his hand again and squeezed it. "I bet Frank, my scarecrow brother-in-law, could get you a job. He owns two gas stations now. Two! He's bound to have something for you."

"But I can't stay. We...our family is different from yours. We don't put down roots in any one place for long. It's not safe." He glanced away and refused to make eye contact for a few seconds. When he did look back at me, his expression was one of surrender. But not to me.

He wasn't joking—Harmon really was leaving. I was hurt that he was going and hurt that he hadn't been honest with me about his family.

"I don't understand what you mean! Why can't you stay? If you're making fun of me, Harmon Gates, I am never going to forgive you. Never!"

I got mad so quickly that I surprised myself. I had no idea I was yelling until the crowd around us began to push back and watch us. I brushed against someone's shoulder, but I couldn't say whose because there were tears in my eyes. I walked away from the first boy who had ever told me that he loved me. Did I love him? How could I know that yet? I'd only just met him! Aunt Dot met me at the punch bowl. Obviously, she hadn't seen us arguing on the dance floor. I guessed she had other things to keep her occupied.

"Oh my. You look pale, Loxley. Are you okay?"

"No, I'm not okay," I said, shaking my head at her. At first, I refused the punch and wiped the tears from my eyes. Then I picked it off the table and stared into the liquid.

"What is it? Would you like to go home? I can tell the principal that I'm leaving. I'm sure he won't mind. There are so many chaperones here tonight."

I bit my lip as I held the drink in my hand. I didn't want to drink it. I wanted to throw it at Harmon, but I didn't do any such thing. "No, I think I'll go for a walk, is all. Just to clear my head. I'm okay, Aunt Dot. I promise."

"Would you like to talk about it?"

Strangely enough, I did want to talk about it, but there was a line forming behind me. A line of thirsty students, or maybe they were just nosy and wanted to know the latest gossip about Aunt Dot and Coach Patrick or me and Harmon Gates. Well, they could eat their hearts out because I wasn't going to give them any information.

I shook my head and pretended to sip my punch while Coach came to "help" cute Aunt Dot deliver cup after cup of prom punch. It was easy to slip out of the gym unnoticed. Thankfully, Harmon was nowhere to be found. Maybe he got the picture. Maybe it was all a big lie. Another joke on Loxley Belle. He couldn't possibly think I was one of those girls who believed every sob story a guy told her. *This might be our last night together, Loxley. Let's make the most of it.*

Yes, I knew what that meant, and he was wrong about me. I was no s-l-u-t. I stepped outside and walked down the steps. The parking lot was as busy as the gymnasium. Kids were out here too, hanging out, listening to car radios and doing who knows what else.

Two security guards patrolled the parking lot. That wasn't a normal sight on campus. But they were clear out on the other side of the parking lot of at least two hundred cars. They were mostly just laughing and smoking. This prom wasn't just for our school but for all the high schools in the county. There were tons of teenagers here tonight. Funny, as I was thinking about Shannon Bohannan not being the Queen Bee tonight, not a shoo-in for Prom Queen after all, I saw her boyfriend's car. An easy pull on the car door revealed that it was unlocked.

It was wrong to sit in someone's car without being invited, but I liked the feeling, that old familiar feeling that I was doing something wrong. It made me stronger. Very carefully, so as to not draw attention to myself, I closed the door. The car light went off, and I sat in darkness for a minute. I could just imagine Chuck and Shannon riding to the prom in this monster of a car. It wasn't nearly as nice as Harmon's, and it smelled like Shannon's perfume. What was I doing? Why had I done such a thing? *Well, while I'm here, I may as well look around.* My dress would wrinkle if I sat too long, and I was already tired of the scratchy petticoat beneath my skirt. There wasn't much to see in here...but the glove box, that might hold a few surprises.

Inside the glove box was a small bottle, no, a flask. Like the kind one would carry if one were to take sips from it during church services as Mr. Watley used to do after collecting the offering. Everyone knew he was drinking booze from that flask, but no one ever said anything. They'd certainly talk about me if they knew what I was up to, though. I closed the glove box, the flask still in my hand. I'd been so focused on plundering that I hadn't noticed the footsteps as they came up beside the vehicle.

Suddenly the door opened, and Shannon Bohannan's boyfriend was staring at me.

Chapter Thirteen—Loxley

I stared at Chuck, unsure what to say. I hadn't planned on being caught, and he was now demanding to know why I was sitting in his car. Shannon was right behind him, looking as furious as ever, and I was terrified. I had no idea what to say or how to explain myself. "What exactly are you doing in here? What kind of mischief are you up to, Loxley Belle?" That was Shannon's nasally voice, but Chuck didn't look happy either.

"I......"

"There you are. Wrong car, toots. It's right over here. Excuse us," Harmon said as he pushed past Chuck and reached for my hand. I kept the flask squirreled beneath my skirt. No way could I put it back now, not that I had ever planned to do so.

"Just a damn minute. Your crazy girlfriend doesn't have any right to climb around in my car. Unless of course she realizes what a loser her date has turned out to be. Is that it, Crazy Belle?"

"I'm not crazy!" I shouted at him. Out of my peripheral vision, I could see the two security officers making their way toward us.

I wasn't the only one. Chuck saw them too and whispered in a low voice, "You two losers need to make like eggs and scram. Hit the road! Or should I call those officers over here?"

"Hey, it was an honest mistake. Our cars are the same color. You know how girls are. They couldn't tell you one make and model from another, right?" Harmon said with a grin at me, but I only frowned at him. I wasn't stupid and didn't appreciate his making fun of me. He elbowed me as Shannon leaned across Chuck's shoulder. She wasn't believing any of this, and I suddenly felt worried. Not so much for me but for Harmon. He'd hinted earlier that he was in some sort of trouble, or at least his family was. I decided to play along and clutched his hand.

"I just wasn't paying attention. Sorry about that, Chuck."

The tall boy tilted his head and looked down at us as if we were two bugs he wanted to crush beneath his dress shoes. He didn't speak to me—I guess he thought he was too good for that—but said to Harmon, "You need to take your nutjob girlfriend and your wheels and get out of here. We don't want your kind here. You two deserve each other."

"You need to take that back. You call her crazy or a nutjob one more time and see what happens to you. You're about to get a fat lip, buddy!"

"Please, Harmon. Let's go. I'd like to get out of here. It was my mistake. It was an honest mistake. We are leaving." I snatched my hand away as I surreptitiously hid the flask in my voluminous skirts.

Shannon Bohannan's boyfriend was cussing up a storm, which actually helped us out because the officers were more worried about his foul language than what I could possibly be doing plundering his car. Harmon's face said it all. He was livid, but with me or Chuck or Shannon... I didn't know.

"I'm sorry I got you into trouble. I don't know what I was thinking."

Harmon took his keys out of his pocket and opened his door, then reached across the seat and unlocked my door. I was still apologizing as I got into his car.

"What were you doing in that car? You know the difference between a Chevy Bel Air and a Buick Roadmaster. What were you doing in there?"

Maybe this was a mistake. Maybe I should go find my aunt and insist that she take me home, but I couldn't move from the vehicle. Knowing that Harmon was furious with me made me feel sick. He was my only friend left in the world, and even if he was leaving soon, I couldn't afford to lose another friend. "I was just looking around."

"Were you looking for something to steal?"

I was flabbergasted that he'd guessed so correctly. "No. Yes, but I can explain everything."

Harmon cranked the vehicle, and we slung out of the school parking lot. Rocks flew as his wheels spun out of the driveway. That was one sure way to draw attention, but at this point, I didn't have any desire to give him driving instructions. "You don't have to explain, but I want you to tell me the truth."

"I don't think you would understand. I hardly understand it myself. What do you want me to say, Harmon? I told you I was crazy. You didn't believe me, but now you know the truth. I am what they say I am. Just like my Momma, I'm a nutjob. A crazy person. A psychopath who steals things. What else do you want to know? And why do you care? You're not even going to be here. You're leaving. Remember?"

I expected him to argue with me. I thought perhaps he might even go as far as to say I wasn't like my mother, that I wasn't a nutjob, but he didn't. His eyes were fixed on his rearview mirror. "Someone is following us, Loxley. Why would they be following us? I think this is going to be bad."

I'd forgotten all about the flask I was still clutching in my right hand. Might as well tell the truth. He knew the worst about me already. I held the flask up and showed it to him. "Because I took this."

"Hells bells, Loxley! We've got to get out of here. The cops are going to come find us. What made you want to steal from that guy's car? You know he's a jerk!"

I felt as stiff as a board as I sat beside Harmon and did my best to think things through. I'd made a real mess of things, such a bad mess that I had put my friend in a horrible position. I glanced over my shoulder and could see the car closing in on us. I couldn't be sure, but the headlights looked familiar. Was it possible that Chuck and Shannon were tailing us? Of course they were. Why else would they have come out to his car except to retrieve that flask? There was a strict no-drinking rule at any school function, but people like Chuck always found ways around those rules.

I knew that I should feel bad, that I should feel guilty for what I'd done, but suddenly I didn't. I felt strong. I felt like I was fighting back against the people who hated me, who enjoyed tearing down my reputation and destroying my family's name. In a surprisingly calm voice, I said to Harmon, "Head east on 98. I know where we can go. I know where we will be safe."

And without question, Harmon drove faster, barreling down the dark highway toward Summerleigh.

I was going home.

Chapter Fourteen—Jerica

"On your way?" I asked hopefully as I picked up the phone without bothering to say hello. I didn't want to sound desperate, but I was beginning to feel that way. After seeing the room destroyed and hearing the scream, not to mention watching the baby's carrier slide across the floor, I was done trying to keep it all together.

"No, unfortunately. My truck bit the dust."

I rubbed my lip as I stared out the kitchen window. "What? Were you in an accident?"

"Nothing like that, sweetheart. It just wouldn't turn over, and then the battery died...it's been a nightmare. But I had it towed from the hotel parking lot and am on the way to the mechanic's shop now. I'm just about ready to say keep the damn thing." Wow, that was big news. Jesse loved his vintage truck, so much so that he'd spent at least one weekend a month tinkering with it. "If they can't fix it in a timely manner, I'll grab a rental car and head that way."

I sighed and closed my eyes. "No, don't do that. You love Old Bruiser. You know you would never abandon him like that. I can't come get you, though. We have guests." *And there really are ghosts in the house, Jesse. I think Loxley is here.*

He laughed softly, and then it was his turn to sigh. "I guess you're right. How are the guests? Nice people, I'm hoping?"

"Yes, they're great. About to head out for the day, I think. There's a big concert in the park in Lucedale. I had no idea that it was such a big deal. I wonder how they're going to get by without the great Jesse Clarke's performance."

He snorted and sounded a bit unimpressed with my attempt at humor. Jesse wasn't the best guitarist or vocalist, but he did love it; at least he was pretty to look at. I reminded myself that he was a bit sensitive about his playing.

"I'm sure they aren't missing me. I better go. Looks like the mechanic wants to talk to me. Well, there goes the profit from this book signing."

"Just let me know how it goes, will you?"

"I will. Bye, Jerica."

"Bye," I said as I put the phone back on the receiver.

I chewed on my fingernail as I thought about the situation. I took the biscuits out of the oven and arranged the small plates on the tray. Breakfast would be simple this morning. As a tribute to Harper, I added a small jar of peach preserves to the tray with a tiny silver spoon. I put the tray on the table with some napkins and headed to the back porch. There were two round tables out here with comfortable chairs. I loved serving breakfast out here. My four guests hurried into the kitchen and walked through to join me on the porch.

"Who wants coffee?" I asked the excited group, and everyone raised their hands. I hurried off to fill a carafe and fetch the cups, but I wasn't alone.

"Excuse me, Jerica. I found this in the bathroom. I figured you left it in there when you were cleaning." Trisha dropped Loxley's charm bracelet in my open hand, and I nearly hit the floor.

"Hey, are you okay? You look like someone just kicked the wind out of you."

"Yes, thank you," I said with a smile even though my hands were shaking and my heart was pounding. I lifted the carafe off the table.

"Let me take that, please. Are you sure you're feeling alright?"

I smiled even bigger. "I'm great, Trisha. Thanks for asking."

The breakfast was like most, over quickly, and there were lots of compliments on the biscuits. As I always did, I gave Harper Belle credit and offered the ladies copies of the recipe if they wanted them. Nobody said no. I returned with pre-printed cards and began tidying up the dishes. I was anxious for them to leave. I had to clean up Loxley's room and figure out how that bracelet ended up in that bathroom.

"We better load up. The first group starts in thirty minutes. We won't be back for lunch, but we will see you tonight, Jerica. Thanks for a wonderful breakfast."

"You're welcome, Mr. Beckett. Would you like me to tidy up your rooms? Need fresh linens?"

"That would be wonderful. I'll go grab the keys, then," Harry said. Karen and Ron followed him through the kitchen, but Trisha lingered behind.

"I think you should know that I saw the girl that bracelet belonged to. I couldn't keep it. I'm guessing that you'll know what to do with it."

I let the hot water run in the sink and added some soap. "Are you a medium?"

"Not really, not a psychic medium, but sometimes I can feel things. Usually when I hold objects or visit certain places.

It doesn't happen reliably enough for me to call myself a real psychic, but if there is anything I can do to help you, please say the word."

I eased the cups into the soapy water and pretended, as best I could, that there wasn't a thing wrong.

"Let me help," she said.

Before I could discourage her, her husband returned and said, "I'm ready when you are, Trisha."

"I think I'm going to stay here. I'm not feeling too well. Another migraine, I think. The idea of sitting in the hot sun all day worries me."

Harry frowned but didn't go against her. "If you think it's best. How about I call you at lunch? If you think you're up to coming out, I'll come back and pick you up. It's not that far away. How does that sound?"

"Wonderful. In the meantime, I'll take a migraine pill and see if I can nip it in the bud. Thanks, Harry."

The three of them left; Karen seemed disappointed but not enough to stay behind. I was glad, too, because I didn't like the idea of creating a panic over a lost bracelet. I wasn't even sure that I wanted to talk about it with Trisha, but she kind of didn't ask me. In some ways, she reminded me of Renee. I glanced at the clock over the phone. Renee was bringing Jordan home in a few hours. She was half asleep when I called a while ago. According to her, Jordan slept through the night, but Frank's snoring kept her up for most of it.

Trisha and I washed dishes in silence. Imagine washing dishes with a stranger. But she was quiet and polite, and when we'd dried the dishes and returned them to the cabinet, we sat on the back porch.

"May I hold the bracelet again?" she asked hopefully. "I think I can tell you more. Especially now that we're alone."

I couldn't say why, but I felt as if I could trust her. I removed the charm bracelet from my pocket. "Here you go," I said as I put it in her hand.

"She's a girl with dark blond hair. Her name...oh dear. She's being shy now. She doesn't want to tell me her name because she thinks she is in trouble. Bad...really bad...she says. She deserved it, she says. She deserved what he did to her because she'd been so bad."

I waited patiently, but I was dying to know who she was talking about. I decided to ask her a question. "Is she young or old?"

"She's young, a teenager. Please tell me your name. We won't tell anyone." Trisha's voice softened as she spoke with the invisible girl. "L....something with an L. She's not being very forthcoming with any of it."

"Loxley...it has to be Loxley."

Trisha began to cry as she clutched the bracelet. "She doesn't want to talk about it. Oh, God, Jerica. She's devastated. So very sad. Please, we have to let her go. She wants to leave." She opened her eyes and put the bracelet on the table.

Suddenly, the screen door slapped shut and I nearly jumped out of my seat at the sound. Trisha didn't seem surprised at all. Maybe I'd left the door open earlier? It was possible. "She wants you to follow her. She's going that way. Can you see her?"

"No, I can't."

Trisha sighed and said, "She wants to show you something—I'll take you. It's not far from here."

"Thank you," I said as we left the porch and walked past the circular driveway and toward the narrow path. I knew exactly where we were going, but there was no way my guest could know. It's not like we handed out maps to visitors. And the discovery of the shack was so new that would have been impossible.

"It's this way." Trisha was practically running, and I was right behind her. Before I knew it, we were standing in front of the shack. Trisha said, "He's in there."

I glanced at her and said with some surprise, "He? I thought we were following Loxley?"

"We were, but he's here and she left. I wish I knew why." She dropped the bracelet in my hand. "He comes back here a lot, and he's looking for her. He won't let her go. She's not at rest, Jerica. Not by any stretch of the imagination."

That's when I saw the shadow move past the window. I walked up the steps and waved at her to stay back. Unfortunately, I couldn't go inside. Jesse had locked the door, and the shiny new doorknob wasn't going to budge.

I turned to speak to Trisha, but she was backing away from the building. Her face was pinched and worried. "I have to go. I'm sorry." She wasn't looking at me but at the window. Although I couldn't see what she was seeing, I knew it was something terrifying because she was running back to Summerleigh.

With the bracelet in my pocket, I ran back too.

Chapter Fifteen—Loxley

"Wait a second," I said as the car went around us and zipped down the highway. "That wasn't them at all. It's all clear, Harmon," I said as I breathed a sigh of relief and sank into the leather seat.

"Good, that's good. Say, what's in that flask? I bet it's high-dollar stuff. Probably Jim Beam. Pass it here." He wasn't turning around, and his eyes never left the road. I did as he asked but felt sure that at any moment he would turn the car around and we would head back to the school, or maybe he'd take me home. Aunt Dot would be expecting me for sure. "Will you unscrew the top for me?"

I took the flask back and unscrewed the top. Harmon took a sip and choked a little. "I should have known better. That's moonshine. Straight-up moonshine. And not good moonshine either. Take a sip."

"No, I don't want any. Where are we going?"

"To Summerleigh. That's where you wanted to go, right? I'd like to go with you."

"Yeah, but that was before, when I thought Chuck and Shannon were following us. I think I should get back."

Harmon took another swig and handed me the flask. "I'll take you home, but can't we at least take a look around? I mean, we're practically there."

I remembered that Harmon told me he had visited the house before, purely by accident, but I was getting a case of the cold chills. I rubbed my arms to try to warm up.

"Here, take my jacket," he said as he shifted around and removed his jacket before I could even say no. I slid it on and pulled it close to me. *Okay, stop being a silly goose. Harmon is your friend, Loxley Belle.* He was right, we would be at Summerleigh in just a few minutes. And I'd been wanting to go, just not with a stranger. *But he's not a stranger.*

"Be careful, Harmon. This road always has potholes after a rain, and you know we had quite a bit of rain last week." Harmon navigated around the potholes as easily as I would have. I hadn't expected that. *Okay, so he knows where the potholes might be. That's not proof that he's been hanging around here, is it?*

It was so dark out here; there were no streetlights on the road behind us or along the driveway. It wouldn't have done any good even if there had been, since the power had been turned off here for years. As the big car jostled us around, I held my breath and waited for us to clear that last turn in the driveway. Even though it was dark, Summerleigh was easy to see. Her massive white walls gave her the appearance of a broken castle. A sand castle with empty windows.

Was that a flash of light upstairs? I thought I saw a candle flicker in the nursery, but then it was gone. Could have been a lightning bug. No, that was much larger than a bug. I didn't have to ask Harmon if he saw the same thing because he was putting the car in park and staring up at the window. But I did anyway.

"You saw it too, didn't you?" I asked in a whisper.

"Yes, but it's gone now. You know how to get inside. I want to see it." He reached for the flask again as he got out of the car. With some misgivings, I followed after him. He'd parked his car right where Momma used to park her Master DeLuxe. Harmon sipped from the flask as he stood on the front porch.

"Not that way," I whispered as I glanced up at the nursery window again. "You have to go through the back."

With a smile, Harmon shuffled down the steps and followed me to the back of Summerleigh. I wasn't embarrassed about the collapsed back porch or the absolutely overpowering smell, not like Momma would have been. "Watch your step, and don't touch anything. Remember, this is my house." I put my hand on the doorknob and fumbled with it until it opened. "One day, I'm coming back to claim what's mine."

"I'll remember. I'll remember."

We walked into the kitchen, and I felt Daddy's presence flee from me. He didn't like that I'd brought a boy here. That must have been it. "Uh, I don't think we should stay long. I do have to go home."

"You said yourself that this was your place. What's the hurry?"

"I don't like it when you try to boss me around."

"Fine, I won't boss you around, toots. Or should I call you thief?" His accusation hurt as much as any slap. "Don't get me wrong, I admire your skills. First a barrette, then a bracelet and now this flask. You could get a few dollars for it. That's sterling silver." He smiled at me as he slipped it into the pocket of the jacket I was still wearing.

"Keep your voice down, Harmon. And I didn't take those things for the money. I don't need any money. I did it because…" I couldn't think why I did it, but it didn't matter anyway. Harmon was opening cabinet doors and completely ignoring my wishes. He was touching everything!

Suddenly, he paused and glanced at me. "Did you say something?"

"I said keep your voice down. And stop touching things."

"No, after that. I thought I heard a woman's voice. Sounds like it came from in here. What's this? The living room?" He walked out of the kitchen, and I followed him as closely as I could. My high heels clicked on the grimy floor. "Damn, this place is falling down around us."

"Don't swear in here. Daddy…" I swallowed as Harmon squinted at me in the dark. "My father never liked us to swear in the house. Momma wouldn't tolerate swearing either."

"Isn't he dead? And I know that she died recently, but you are your own person, Loxley. Practically a woman."

Harmon's indifference to my mother's recent death disturbed me. "What do you mean practically? I am a woman, but I still like to follow their wishes," I said as I thrust my chin up at him defiantly.

"Okay, no swearing. Let's check out the rest of the house."

"Go ahead," I said as I watched him walk to the front room and head toward the far hallway. I felt very uncomfortable all of a sudden. We weren't alone at Summerleigh, and Harmon wasn't at all cognizant of that fact. And that was bad news.

Loxley…

I saw legs disappearing up the staircase. But whose? They moved too quickly for me to tell, but they were young. And bare. Without waiting for Harmon, I walked up the stairs a few steps to get a better glimpse. I could think of only one person who would run up and down the stairs bare-legged. Not the horrid Ghost Boy or the Lady in White. Not Daddy or any of the other occasional visitors, the dead who just happened to be passing by Summerleigh.

Those legs belonged to my sister. After all this time, I knew the truth. My sister Jeopardy was dead. She'd never left us. I gasped as I clutched my chest and my corsage rubbed against my skin. I suddenly felt very vulnerable to the spirits of Summerleigh. Even though she was my sister, I felt cold and kind of sick.

"Jeopardy? Is that really you?"

I walked up the stairs slowly, taking my time to clear each and every step. As I stood on the landing, I heard bare footsteps again. Running sounds, running down the hall, but my eyes could see nothing in the darkness. I heard the jacks tapping in the nursery—the Ghost Boy was here too, but he wanted nothing to do with me. I was too grown, too old for him. But then I saw the attic door close, Jeopardy's castle room door.

What could I do but walk toward it?

I heard heavy footsteps coming up the stairs behind me and assumed it was Harmon. Who else could it be?

Stomp, stomp, stomp.

"This way, Harmon," I whispered into the darkness. "But stay back. Please, stay back." I waved my free hand behind me, and he took it. His icy grip surprised me, so much so that I snatched my hand back. Then I realized that Harmon wasn't there. He was downstairs calling me.

Dread rose up within me, but I continued on. I had to see my sister. It had been so long, and just knowing she was here...I had to see her face. Tell her I love her.

As I reached for the doorknob, the door began to shake so hard that I thought it would come off the hinges. It didn't, but it could have. I stepped back and watched it until it stopped. Harmon was with me now.

"What is it? What's going on?"

I didn't answer him. He was the one who wanted to be here. He wanted to see the place for himself. So be it.

I turned the knob, and the door swung open with a creak.

I heard Harmon's muffled swearing behind me. "We're not alone, Loxley. Look, I knew they were following us." He touched my arm, and I could see the car lights easing down the driveway toward us.

Could be Aunt Dot or the police. But I knew in my heart that it wasn't.

"Where's a good place to hide?"

"Follow me," I said as I dragged him into the attic and shut the door behind us. Even in the dark, I knew where to go. Behind the armoire, the one beside the trunk. These items both belonged to the Lady in White, but I didn't figure she'd mind. Hopefully.

It didn't take long for us to hear the footsteps coming up the stairs.

Chapter Sixteen—Loxley

"It's totally spooky up here. You got a flashlight or something?" That was Shannon's voice—I'd recognize it anywhere. High, nasally and as always condescending.

Chuck snapped back a snarky response, "You don't have one in your purse? Or in your non-existent bosom? Let's just go. We're never going to find them."

"Shut up, jerk face, and look around. I may not have a flashlight, but I've got a weapon. Those two have got to be up here somewhere. Come out, come out, wherever you are...come out, Crazy Belle." Shannon's voice had a sing-songy sound to it, but it wasn't pleasant. I didn't for a minute believe she wanted to just hang out. Chuck slammed a door, and I heard a weird shuffling.

Oh, God. Please don't let them find us.

I could see them both through the crack in the armoire door. Chuck flicked a lighter and held it up like a candle. It made a tall flame, and Shannon whined when he got too close. "You're going to set me on fire if you aren't careful. Keep looking."

Chuck didn't say much except, "You sure are bitchy for someone who won a crown tonight. Cut the gas. I have to find that flask—it's my old man's."

"Keep your voice down, stupid. Let's just go. Your old man won't care about that stupid bottle."

Chuck kicked over a pile of blankets. "It's a flask, and you don't know my old man."

I heard a sound beside me, muffled but definitely a noise. And then I felt him. The Ghost Boy. His cold hand was on my arm, and his dark eyes were boring into mine. I could see those two pits of darkness even in the blackness. I tried to pull away from him, but he wasn't turning me loose. And then to make things more terrifying, he leaned toward me and opened his mouth as if he would bite me.

"No!" I screamed as I tumbled out of the armoire. The boy's icy grip loosened as I revealed myself to the two intruders.

"Well, look who it is, Chuck. It's our very own Crazy Belle. I should have known you'd be hiding like a scared rabbit. And in a closet, no less," Shannon said sarcastically. Now that my eyes had adjusted to the darkness, I could see her smirk perfectly. That or perhaps I had seen it too many times. I would recognize that smirk anywhere. "Where are his flask and my bracelet? You better cough them up, or I'll make you regret ever stealing from us!"

I glanced over my shoulder, but the Ghost Boy had vanished, no doubt happy that I had revealed my location to my tormentors. *What had I ever done to him? Except be his friend?*

I stepped to the side, just to get closer to the door, but Chuck must have known what I was thinking because he was quick to block my way. He waved the lighter around, but the flame went out and apparently burned him; he yelped as the room went dark. The only light now was what filtered through the nearby dirty window. Chuck's lighter clattered to the ground.

"Stop fumbling around with that lighter and don't let her out!" Shannon griped as she nearly tripped over something she hadn't seen. Probably one of my treasure boxes. She'd never find that bracelet, and I was never going to give it to her. Not now, not ever. I thought I heard footsteps not far away, but Harmon never emerged.

What's his plan? What do we do now? This is all my fault.

"I swear something bumped me, knocked the lighter out of my hand. Let's get out of here. Grab her arm," Chuck ordered Shannon. They both reached for me, but I ducked and stepped over the small box on the floor. It didn't do me much good. "No way, Crazy Belle. I've got you now."

Suddenly there was a banging and clattering, and Harmon stepped out of the shadows. "Get your hands off of her. Leave her alone!"

Chuck laughed at him and instead of obeying Harmon's command gripped my wrist and pulled me close to him. "Well, now the other rabbit comes out of hiding. You were just going to let her suffer? Some kind of man. Maybe she should get to know a real man."

I didn't know exactly what Chuck meant by that last statement, but I felt sick and my arm felt like it was going to break from his twisting.

Shannon's voice dropped as if someone might hear us. "Now, let's everyone calm down. I'm here for my property. What are you here for, Chuck?"

"My property, and I'm not leaving without it."

Shannon reached down and picked up the lighter gingerly. "Shut up, fool. Now look, we don't care about you and Crazy Belle and whatever you're doing here, but we want our stuff.

My bracelet and his flask. If you don't tell us where they are, you'll regret it."

Moving like a cat, Harmon cleared the distance between him and Chuck; I thought for sure there was a full-on fight coming, but out of nowhere Shannon raced toward Harmon with a small shiny object in her hand.

The knife! She really did have a knife!

He screamed, and blood poured from the side of his face. Everyone's attention was drawn to Harmon, who was tackling Chuck and pushing Shannon to the side. "Loxley, run!"

Chuck wasn't playing fair, and Harmon's face was good and bloody now. How could he see? Shannon was screaming but was quickly recovering and getting back up for the next round. Whatever that would look like.

"Loxley, I said run!"

Shannon was running toward me but tripped again. How did that box get there? Then I felt a hand tug on mine, a small, warm hand, and I smelled a familiar perfume. Kind of like wildflowers. *Jeopardy!*

"Harmon," I sobbed as my dead sister pulled me to the door. I thought Shannon would chase me, but she was focused on Harmon. I didn't see the knife in her hands anymore at least. I wanted to help him, but I had to run. He wanted me to run. And Jeopardy was here, her wild hair flying behind her. I was taller than her—Jeopardy was so young.

"Jeopardy," I whimpered as Harmon screamed from the attic. "They're killing him!" She didn't pause or stop, but I felt her hand continue to pull me down the stairs and toward the parlor. And then she was gone. Disappeared.

"Jeopardy!" I yelled, my eyes now blurry with tears.

Run, stupid!

I ran out of the kitchen, through the rotten porch and outside. The moon cast a muted light on the overgrown yard, and I could hear the ruckus still going on upstairs.

Harmon, I'm coming back for you, I promise!

I raced to his car, praying to God above that he'd left the keys there, but they weren't to be found. I tripped over my high heel as I hurried to Chuck's car to search it for keys. I had no better luck. Wherever I was going, I was going on foot.

"Where are you, Crazy Belle? I've got something for you! I want my bracelet! You can run, but I'll find you. I swear I'll find you, and it will be worse for you!"

Then everything went silent. Harmon wasn't screaming anymore, and Shannon stopped calling to me. The only sound I heard was whippoorwills calling to one another. And Jeopardy's voice again.

Run, stupid.

And I did.

Chapter Seventeen—Loxley

The tin roof on Daddy's hideaway shone like a beacon in the moonlight. Jeopardy was nowhere to be found, and I had nowhere else to go. I could hear Shannon still calling my name in that strange sing-songy voice. "Harmon," I sobbed in a whisper as I made for the shed. There were no lights on; this place never had electricity. There were gas lamps inside, but no way could I take a risk by lighting one. That would make it too easy for Shannon and Chuck to find me. And if they'd done to Harmon what I imagined, if they'd killed him, then they wouldn't hesitate to kill me too.

"Run, Crazy Belle! We'll find you! We want our property back, thief!" Shannon's voice hung in the air; they had to be close now. Too close for comfort.

I hurried up the steps, not even thinking that the shack might be locked. Fortunately for me, it wasn't. It creaked slightly as I jerked the door open. Clouds of dust met me as I stepped inside and closed the door behind me. The oversized desk, the desk that Daddy built, was exactly where he left it. The desktop was covered with boxes—lots of boxes, full of Daddy's mementos from the war. I remembered the day Momma and Harper loaded them in the car to bring them out here. For the life of me, I couldn't figure out why Momma would do such a thing. Why would she want to get rid of Daddy's things? Summerleigh was big enough to hide a hundred boxes, but she wanted them out of the house. Daddy's ghost hadn't been too happy about it, but I couldn't tell Momma. She loved me best when I pretended that I didn't see my dead father.

But Momma and Harper had gotten into a knock-down, drag-out over Jeopardy's things. "No, Momma. She's coming back! We can't get rid of her stuff." On this, Momma relented, but Daddy's stuff? It had to go. When the two of them had returned about a half an hour later, Harper's face was an unemotional mask, but Momma was as happy as a lark. There was no time now to dig through these forgotten treasures, but I would have to do that. How could I have forgotten them?

I didn't forget, Daddy. Not really.

Where to hide? There was only one room and no closets. The space beneath the desk wouldn't hide me for long. It was the largest piece of furniture in the place—they were sure to look there first. I paced the small area, scanning the darkness for a safe place to hide. It had to be here because I could hear them coming and this little building had no exit door. I couldn't get to the windows; they were blocked with boxes and junk.

As I walked, I noticed that the floorboards squeaked beneath me. I suddenly remembered a long-ago afternoon of following Jeopardy around. I had been a notorious lurker. Tagalong was the name Jeopardy called me. Of all my sisters, I enjoyed following her the most. I think she knew that I followed her, but unlike Harper, she never shoved me in a closet or commanded me to go home.

Falling to my knees, I began prying up that loose floorboard. It came up easily, followed by three more. Beneath me there was a gaping black hole, probably full of biting creatures like spiders and snakes. Poisonous, creepy spiders at that. I hated them the most. But my adrenaline was pumping, and I had to survive. Not just for me but for Harmon. He needed my help, and I'd run away like a coward. I had to return to Summerleigh.

Harmon, I'm coming back for you!

Without another thought, I descended into the darkness and dragged the boards in place over me. Nobody would know I was here. How could they? Daddy had dug this hole before he laid the first boards down. I bumped into a glass bottle, probably one of Daddy's forgotten moonshine jugs. I got very still so as not to make any further sounds, and just in time too. They were here! The dark, dusty space smelled terrible—like no fresh air had ever passed through here and something had slowly decayed beneath these floorboards. *Oh, God! Please don't let anything dead be down here! Especially not the Ghost Boy.* But it wouldn't be the Ghost Boy. He never left Summerleigh. Or at least I'd never seen him out here.

I was breathing so hard that I wondered how I would ever remain hidden. Shannon and Chuck's footsteps were so loud on the porch—obviously, they weren't worried about surprising me.

"Come out, come out wherever you are, Crazy Belle," I heard Shannon taunting me as she and her meathead boyfriend surveyed the ramshackle room. I didn't answer, and I could hear Shannon let out an aggravated sigh. "She's not here!" Her high heels tapped on the floor—she was right above me. I could hear the fabric of her expensive skirt and smell her aggressive perfume. With closed eyes and clenched fists, I held my breath and counted in my head. *One Mississippi. Two Mississippi. Three Mississippi...* I wondered how many Mississippis would pass before she left. Thirty? Because I could hold my breath for about that long. *Calm down, Loxley Belle. This is like playing hide-and-seek with your sisters, that's all.* Although I never really played...more like I followed my sisters around and revealed their hiding places.

What if the Ghost Boy reappeared? How long could I keep quiet then? I needed to breathe—I was never good at holding my breath, not like Jeopardy or Harper. But I could always beat Addison, who was lousy at any type of outdoor activity like swimming.

My two tormentors were arguing loudly. Shannon didn't want to keep searching for me, but Chuck was determined to recover his flask. "Give me your knife."

"Why? What are you going to do with it?" Shannon asked nervously as she stepped toward the desk where Chuck sat. I could hear the sound of them kissing, which made me sick to my stomach. I couldn't hold my breath any longer. Releasing the air from my lungs as quietly as I could, I took another deep breath and held it.

"Did you hear that?" Shannon asked.

Chuck had been scratching with his knife; I could hear the blade digging into the wood. He paused his evil work but only for a few seconds. "I didn't hear anything. Probably squirrels or rats."

Shannon wasn't listening to him. She was walking back toward me again. I thought she would squat down and spot me, look me right in the eye, but she didn't. Suddenly she turned on her heel and said, "I'm bored with this. Let's go back to the dance. I've got a midnight curfew, remember?"

"Just a second—we have plenty of time. It's nowhere near midnight. I'm just leaving a little note for Crazy Belle."

"Ooh, let me see." I heard her laughing softly, and then they were kissing again. "She's never going to see that, Chuckie. Nobody comes out here; it looks like the place has been untouched since Crazy Belle's father died."

"Okay, I'm done. But I left my jacket in the house, and I wouldn't mind asking that punk about my flask again. I'm telling you, my old man is going to pitch a fit when he finds out I've lost it. He warned me, and now he's going to make me pay for it. Do you know what that means, Shannon? My old man is going to kick my ass." He mumbled something else, but I couldn't hear what he said.

Shannon walked to the door, her dainty heels echoing beneath the floors. "You're going to kill him if you're not careful. And look...you've got blood on your cuff." Shannon didn't really sound as if she cared one way or another, but I had to stop them. Poor Harmon! No more hiding. I had to save my friend!

Before I could scream at them or move a muscle or do anything else, a small hand covered my mouth. With wide eyes, I turned my head ever so slightly to see Jeopardy beside me.

She had her finger to her mouth, and her voice was in my head.

Keep quiet, stupid.

Tears rolled down my face as I waited for them to leave.

Jeopardy? It really is you, isn't it?

Although the sight of her comforted me for the moment, I was heartsick. The sight of her gray, flickering image tore my soul in two. Jeopardy really was dead. She was dead and never coming home to us. Never. Ever.

Jeopardy, you can't be dead. Please, tell me you aren't dead. Come home, Jeopardy!

She must have heard my thoughts because she answered me the same way.

Bring me home, Loxley. I want to come home.

Jeopardy sighed and vanished, leaving me alone in the cold, dark space beneath the floor.

Chapter Eighteen—Loxley

Jeopardy left me quite alone. One second, her hand covered my mouth; the next, she wasn't there at all. There was no one there, and I knew for absolute certain that Jeopardy Belle was surely dead. And not only dead but lost. My two terrorists had left, and now my sister was gone too. They had barely left the shed when I was pushing up floorboards and climbing out of the dirt like a raving lunatic. Then again, only a lunatic—a Crazy Belle—would hide in the floor. I couldn't catch my breath, but I had to get hold of myself. I had to, for Harmon's sake. I shuffled to the window and peered outside. The woods surrounding the shed were dark; there wasn't a trace of light, not even moonlight.

But I couldn't let that stop me. As I reached for the door, I heard a clunking sound. My toe struck something metal. I reached down to pick it up. I knew that symbol—it was the school's monogram, something only seniors could own. It was silver and shiny. I clutched it in my hand.

A keychain! These must be Chuck's keys, and he'd figure out where he left them eventually. I had to hurry. If I could get to the car, I could get help from somewhere! The Richardsons lived just down the road.

I stumbled coming down the steps. I was grateful that Aunt Dot had encouraged me to go with the lower heels tonight. This fall could have killed me. I was sweating beneath

Harmon's jacket. The flask in the jacket pocket felt heavy—like it weighed a hundred pounds. Like my own guilt, it weighed so heavily on my soul. Would my evil ways cost Harmon his life? I had known for a long time that Shannon Bohannan hated me, but I'd barely had a conversation with Chuck. Did everyone at school call me Crazy Belle behind my back?

The race back to the driveway seemed longer than ever, and when I got there, I could hear Chuck swearing. He must have discovered that his keys were missing, and sooner than I expected. Shannon berated him as she leaned against the car with her arms crossed.

"You're such a lug nut, Chuck Welford. How could you do something so stupid?"

As he pulled himself out of the car, he snapped back at her, "This was your idea, wasn't it? Make yourself useful and help me find them. Are you thick or something? Do you want to spend the night here? Is that what you want?"

I watched as she stomped her foot at him. "You better take me home right now, Chuck."

"Again, are you thick or something? Without the keys, we aren't going anywhere. Start looking."

Shannon began scanning the ground, complaining the whole time. "This would be easier if we had a flashlight. When was the last time you had the keys? There's an entire forest to search."

"If I knew where they were...what the hell? Did you see that?"

"What?" Shannon asked fearfully as she hurried to the open driver's side door. "What is it? A ghost or something?

They say this place is haunted by Crazy Belle's dad. I've always heard that."

"No, listen!"

Harmon Gates staggered out the front door and practically fell on the ground. I could hear him crying, asking for help, begging, but there was nothing I could do.

Except wait. And maybe somehow atone for the sin that put him in this position. I slipped my hand into the pocket of Harmon's jacket and closed my fingers around the flask. Slowly and quietly, I pulled it out and set it gently in the overgrowth. I didn't want Chuck to find it, but I couldn't carry it with me. Not anymore.

Chuck stumbled toward him with Shannon close behind. I suspected that the beating he'd given Harmon had taken something out of him. Harmon moaned and coughed as if he couldn't breathe.

"Hey, creep! Over here! You want some help? I'll help you!"

Shannon reached for Chuck's shoulder, but he flung her hand off. He had one thing on his mind, beating the life out of Harmon. But why? Why did he hate him so? They were ten, then twenty feet away from me. The car door was open, and I had the keys in my hand! Chuck was reaching for Harmon, who sagged beneath his reach like a rag doll.

What now? I couldn't take on both Chuck and Shannon, but I could steal that car! That might be the diversion we needed. I screamed for some ungodly reason as I ran and threw myself inside the vehicle.

"Run, Harmon!"

I fumbled with the keys but managed to get the key into the ignition, slamming the door shut at the same time. I'd only ever driven Aunt Dot's convertible; Chuck's car was a monster compared to her car. I slung the steering wheel and without thinking shifted to first gear instead of reverse. Slamming the gas, I screamed again as the bumper whacked Shannon. Her screams tore through the night air as I put the vehicle in reverse. The moonlight gave me enough light to see Harmon limping into the woods beside Summerleigh. And then he was gone, but Chuck was pulling on the door handle. I slapped the door lock, shifted into gear and hit the gas as the car took off down the sandy driveway.

I didn't go far, only as far as the Richardsons' house, but it might as well have been a million miles. I threw the car in park and didn't bother turning it off. I wanted to get as far away from the thing as I could. Had I killed Shannon? Was that possible? Could I be a killer too?

"Mrs. Richardson! Please open the door! It's me, Loxley! Mrs. Richardson!"

The old woman cracked the door and peeked outside, but when she saw me, she wasted no time ushering me in. I confessed everything in a rush of words and waited as she dialed the sheriff's office. Mrs. Richardson thrust a glass of water in my hand, and we waited on the porch as a parade of emergency vehicles screamed down Hurlette Drive.

I was still holding the sweaty glass of water when Aunt Dot arrived.

All I could do was watch. Lights swirled, sirens screamed. Then there was a crowd of people in Mrs. Richardson's yard. Some I recognized, some I did not. Their mouths moved. I knew they were talking to me, but I only heard a swirling, swooshing noise. It reminded me of the sound I heard when I put my ear to Jeopardy's giant seashell, the one Daddy sent us Belles. I loved that shell but rarely got a chance to play with it. Jeopardy kept all his gifts in her castle room because Momma liked throwing them away. I could understand why Jeopardy hid them, but I also resented that she was the keeper of all Daddy's precious gifts. No, she never shared Daddy, and now she was gone forever.

Gone with Daddy.

"Gone with Daddy. Gone with Daddy."

Suddenly, Harper's face was in front of me. Her mouth moved too, but I couldn't hear anything. Could she hear me? I began saying it over and over again. "Gone with Daddy! Gone with Daddy! She's gone with Daddy!"

That last sentence must have gotten through because Harper's face crumpled.

"No, Loxley. Take that back. She's not gone. I'm going to bring her home." Harper wasn't kneeling in front of me anymore. She was on her feet, her face pale, her lips quivering. "I promised..."

Fear crept up my spine, and the strange sluggishness vanished. I couldn't daydream now. I had to be alive and in the moment for Harper. And Aunt Dot.

I would have to face up to my crimes, my horrible sins. Now was the time.

I put my arms around Harper as she continued to tremble like a frightened bird. She whispered, "I'm going to bring her home. I promised. Remember? She's not gone."

"I know, I know, Harper." The feeling of Harper's trembling body worried me deeply. Would she have another seizure? Would it be because of me? Because of what I'd done? I couldn't stand to see that. She might not make it through another one.

Please, God. Don't take Harper from me. Forgive me for adding one more sin to my list. After this, no more. I promise. No, I swear, God.

"I didn't see her. You can bring her home, Harper. We'll bring her home together. You hear me? Together." I took Harper by the arms and looked into her eyes.

"Yes, we'll bring her home, Loxley Grace. I promised her I would bring her home."

"We will, Harper. We will," I said as I rubbed her arms gently. That was all I needed. Someone to believe me. And that's what Harper needed too. She needed to believe that she could bring Jeopardy home. We needed to love each other, be there for one another. This feeling, this love, was stronger than any clumsy power I reached for. Stronger than stealing and getting over on the people who hurt me.

Hours later, I was riding in Aunt Dot's car, but we weren't headed home. Not yet. I had to see Harmon, to thank him and tell him I was sorry. Aunt Dot didn't object, and Harper was saying very little but held my hand tight the whole way.

We turned into the pokey George County Hospital driveway, hurried inside and inquired at the hospitality desk. But there was no record of Harmon Gates. Shannon's parents were here. I'd broken her leg with the bumper, but Aunt Dot didn't tolerate their stares for long.

"Let's go home, girls. We'll call the sheriff. We all need to rest. But we'll visit Harmon in the morning, Loxley, I promise."

I was shocked that Harmon wasn't here—he'd been beaten so badly. *Surely he isn't dead! No! Please don't let that be true!* I pulled his jacket tighter around me and cried a little on the way home. When we got there, I was exhausted. I crawled into my bed and fell asleep. When I woke up, Harper was sleeping beside me. I smiled at the sight. She must have come to check on me. She and I both knew we had to look out for one another.

We Belles were a dying breed.

I slid out of bed quietly and reached for my robe. As I walked to the kitchen, I could hear Aunt Dot on the phone. "Are you sure? Where could he have gone? Have you checked the Mobile hospitals? Or the one in Greene County?" After a pause, she said quietly, "Okay, I'll tell her. Yes, we will come see you later. Just a few hours. Thank you, Sheriff."

I leaned against the doorframe as she glanced up. I knew right away what was going on. Harmon Gates was gone. He was gone and I'd never see him again.

Chapter Nineteen—Jerica

With the bracelet safely tucked in my blue jeans pocket and the flask in my back pocket, I dug deeper into the flowerbed. I'd recognized Chuck's stolen property right away when Jesse brought it in the house. He'd been working in the overgrown patch of bushes to the right of the long driveway, so it wasn't a stretch to figure out that was how it came to be there. Loxley must have dropped it while she was watching Chuck and Shannon. I'd cleaned it and polished it up, and thankfully Jesse hadn't asked me about it again. He would eventually, but I had already made up my mind that I wasn't going to tell him anything about what I knew. Loxley didn't need anything from me except to keep her secret. Some secrets shouldn't be shared with the world.

I couldn't be sure this was the exact location I retrieved the recipe box from, but it was as close as I was going to get. The flask was barely going to fit inside it, but if I unscrewed the top, I could make it work. I glanced up at my husband, and thankfully he wasn't paying me any attention. He was too busy loading up his bookshelves and arranging his tchotchkes on his desk. This was something I needed to do alone. Yeah, this one was all on me. I had to do it for Loxley.

I pulled the recipe box out of the tote bag and opened it up. I hadn't kept any of Loxley's treasures. *Your secret is safe with me, Loxley Grace. I am your friend.* I dug the bracelet out of my pocket and placed it inside the recipe box along with the flask. I closed the lid and stroked the metal one last time. *I swear I'll never tell.* I put the box in the open hole and cast dirt over it with my shovel, then leaned back and breathed a sigh of relief. I felt lighter, my spirit confirming that this had been the right thing to do all along. Not all secrets needed to be revealed. The Belles had suffered enough. Maybe, somehow, this would give Loxley the peace she needed. The peace she deserved. And maybe she'd find Harmon.

"Hey! What are you doing out there? Come see!" Jesse's handsome head poked out the window, and I shoved the hand shovel in the dirt.

"Just piddling around, adding a few flowers. On my way," I called back cheerfully. I deposited the bag in the truck and dusted off my legs and went inside. I didn't like lying to Jesse, and I certainly didn't want to be lied to, but this wasn't about us. This was for Loxley.

"Should I close my eyes?" I asked jokingly as I hung in the doorway.

"It's not that big of a surprise. But if you want to close your eyes, I'll do my best to surprise you," he murmured as he took my hand.

"Uh, maybe later," I said with a laugh as he led me to the freshly painted desk. He didn't have to tell me what he'd done. The horrible scratch marks were gone, the threat was gone. The desk had been sanded, and despite our earlier misgivings about covering the wood, it had a nice coat of light blue paint on it and looked beautiful. Jesse and I were wood purists—if we didn't have to paint it, we wouldn't—but this seemed to work. Jesse had gone with a nautical theme for his writer's shack. I liked it. I seriously doubted that I would spend a lot of time here, but as long as he was happy, that's what mattered.

"Jesse, this is perfect. I love it." I rubbed my fingers across the wood where the horrible threat had been. "It's like it never even happened. Did you find out anything about the arrests? Was Chuck ever charged with beating Harmon? What about Shannon?"

He kissed my cheek and handed me an envelope. "This is what I found. I have to admit it's strange to me that you were called on to help the Belles again, but I guess you and Harper will always be connected. I just hoped that it would all come to an end after we found Jeopardy and after we knew the truth about Mariana."

I held his calloused hands and rubbed them lovingly. "I know, I thought so too, but I can't turn away from Loxley. And this time is different. She's not asking us to do anything except keep her secret. I guess she showed me what happened to her because she needed to. I don't know."

"Go ahead and open it," Jesse said in a soft voice.

Curious about what was inside, I slid the papers out; these were copies of old police reports. Not on Chuck Welford or Shannon Bohannan but on Harmon Gates. I flicked on the lamp and sat at the desk. I couldn't believe what I was reading. The charming young man, the boy who declared his love to Loxley Belle, was a criminal.

"He really was a troubled young man, Jerica. He had priors for breaking and entering. Stolen cars. His brother-in-law was a horrible influence. Harmon disappeared before the cops could come cuff him up. Gone without a trace. He didn't even stick around for medical attention since he and his family were on the run. Loxley dodged a bullet, if you ask me."

I stared at the mug shot of Harmon Gates and felt my heart sag within me. Not for me but for Loxley. Had I done the right thing by putting the flask in the box along with the bracelet? I don't know where I got the idea to do such a thing, but I woke up with that on my mind. I'd even seen myself on my knees, the shovel in my hand. I felt better having done it, but that was before I saw this police report.

"Nothing else about him?"

"Nope. It's like he fell off the planet, but that's how these grifters operate. They are masters at vanishing into thin air." Jesse's thick eyebrows furrowed. "He's not haunting the place, is he? Is that why our guests left so quickly this morning?"

"No, he's not haunting the place. Relax, Jess. Everything is okay."

He sighed and picked up the cardboard box. "You ready to head back to Summerleigh? Frank should be there now, and I'm sure Renee would rather spend the afternoon with him than our son."

"Oh, I don't know. Those Clarke boys are pretty irresistible. Did she tell you the news?" I slid my arms around his waist and smiled up at him.

"No, what news?"

"Maybe I should keep it to myself. She wouldn't like me stealing her thunder."

Jesse dropped the box on the desk and stared down at me. "You can't do that. You have to tell me now."

"Fine, but when she tells you, you better act surprised. You, Jesse Clarke, are going to be an uncle. I mean, technically, the baby would be your second cousin, but you know how it works around here. She's Aunt Ree-Ree to Jordan, and you'll be Uncle Jesse to her little one."

He hugged me and laughed. "That's great news. She's always wanted a family. We're family people, for sure. I love mine."

"We love you too. But you're right, we better get back. You can sneak back later and get some writing done. What's your next project? Have you decided yet?"

"Yep, I have a few plans. Fiction, believe it or not. A ghost story."

I breathed him in and closed my eyes. I wanted to remember this moment forever. I had moments like this a lot lately.

I really am blessed. Really and truly. Unlike many of the people who called Summerleigh home before us. I'm sorry, Loxley. Sorry that it didn't work out for you and Harmon.

I opened my eyes just in time to see a young woman squatting near the flowerbed. I didn't move a muscle, didn't let on that I'd seen her. Jesse didn't need to know about this. She stood up, her brown hair sparkling in the sunshine. Her eyes were large and expressive, but she didn't speak to me. Her attention was focused on something beyond my vision. And then he was there. Harmon Gates was next to her, his hand in hers. Nobody had ever smiled bigger than Loxley Belle in this moment. Nobody had ever been happier.

Somehow, she'd showed me how to bring them together. That's what she'd wanted. That was all, and I'd done it. Now everything was quiet. No more ghosts of Summerleigh. The last Belle was happy and free.

And so were we.

Connect with M.L. Bullock on Facebook[1]. To receive updates on her latest releases, visit her website at M.L. Bullock[2] and subscribe to her mailing list. You can also contact her at authormlbullock@gmail.com.

About the Author

Author of the best-selling *Seven Sisters* series and the *Desert Queen* series, M.L. Bullock has been storytelling since she was a child. A student of archaeology, she loves weaving stories that feature her favorite historical characters—including Nefertiti. She currently lives on the Gulf Coast with her family but travels frequently to explore the southern states she loves so much.

---

1. https://www.facebook.com/AuthorMLBullock

2. http://www.mlbullock.com

Don't miss out!

Visit the website below and you can sign up to receive emails whenever M.L. Bullock publishes a new book. There's no charge and no obligation.

https://books2read.com/r/B-A-CXMC-DBQRB

BOOKS 2 READ

Connecting independent readers to independent writers.

Also by M.L. Bullock

Desert Queen Saga
The Tale of Nefret
The Falcon Rises
The Kingdom of Nefertiti
The Song of the Bee Eater

Devecheaux Antiques and Haunted Things Trilogy Series
Devecheaux Antiques and Haunted Things
A Cup of Shadows
A Voice From Her Past
A Watch Of Weeping Angels

Gulf Coast Paranormal Season Two
The Beast of Limerick House

Gulf Coast Paranormal Trilogy Series

Ghosted
Haunted
Dead
Spooked
Paranormal

Haunting Passions
For the Love of Shadows
Her Haunted Heart

Marietta
The Bones of Marietta
Footsteps of Angels

Scary Fall Stories
Horrible Little Things

Seven Sisters
Seven Sisters
Moonlight Falls On Seven Sisters
Ghost on a Swing

Summerleigh
The Belles of Desire, Mississippi
The Ghost Of Jeoprady Belle
The Lady In White
Loxley Belle

Twelve to Midnight
Mary Twelves
Pieces of Twelves

Standalone
Christmas at Seven Sisters
Delivered Me From Evil

Watch for more at www.mlbullock.com.

About the Author

Author M.L. Bullock enjoys the laid-back atmosphere and the spooky vibe of the Gulf Coast, especially the region's historic districts and sites. When she isn't visiting her favorite haunts in New Orleans or Old Mobile, you can find her flipping through old photographs or newspaper clippings in search of new inspiration.

Read more at www.mlbullock.com.